BOOK TWO OF THE YEW TREE CHRONICLES

BLAST INTO THE PAST

BARNABY CREW

Cover Design by www.spiffingcovers.com

ISBN 978-1-9162999-1-7

First published in Great Britain in 2021 by
goldwingpress.com

CHAPTER ONE

'Well … look who it ain't.'

The whining voice carried on the wind to reach Spike's ears, but before he could turn to look, a heavy blow knocked the breath from his chest. Spinning helplessly, he crunched against a wall, pain searing his skin as it scraped along the jagged brickwork.

He threw out an arm to protect himself, shuddering as he felt his hand disappear into a pool of thick, slimy mud.

For a moment, his hand slid wildly along and then he tensed his arm, heaved himself upward, and clutched at the wall, gasping for breath.

'Oh look,' said the voice, now in front of him. 'A pig in muck.'

Spike looked up into a face he recognised. The hair was cropped close, the eyes hooded and dark. Brett Tyler. It was that scumbag, Brett Tyler. The face leered down at him, sniggering like some stupid kid.

Spike's blood began to boil. Why did he have to be here?

Hot with anger, Spike stood up to face him, skidding and sliding, shaking the mud from his hands. It oozed through his fingers and slipped to the ground. 'Only one pig here,' he growled. 'And I'm looking at it.'

He bent down and swiftly scooped up a large handful of the mud, then pulled back his arm to launch it at Brett's smug face.

'Spike!'

Gran's voice stopped him in his tracks. Reluctantly, he lowered his arm, then still glaring at Brett's grinning face, he opened his hand and shook the contents onto the ground, wiping his hand as best he could on a small patch of grass.

'Don't let him goad you.'

Joseph Price had appeared between them. Somehow swallowing his anger, Spike looked up at the man he'd always loved and respected as a grandfather, and he felt the rage subside.

Joseph looked back at him steadily. 'Rise above it,' he said, quietly. 'Use your wits, lad, not your fists.'

He held Spike's gaze for a second and then, dipping into his pocket, Joseph produced a couple of clean handkerchiefs.

'Here, wipe yourself down. And as for you ...'

Swinging around, Joseph took a quick step toward Brett Tyler, who stumbled backwards. 'It's time you put as much effort into helping your aunt as you do causing trouble,' Joseph said. 'It may have escaped your notice, but she could do with some assistance.'

He nodded towards a brightly lit stall, where Brett Tyler's aunt was desperately trying to serve customers. Joseph turned and put a hand on Spike's shoulder, and together they strode away, knowing exactly what Brett Tyler was doing behind their back.

The trip to the Christmas Fair and Market had been Gran's idea.

'Cheer you both up a bit,' she'd said.

It was a trip they made every year, but this year Spike couldn't really be bothered. Truth was, he was finding it hard to be 'bothered' about anything these days. Nothing was the same without dear old Ed.

Ed had been an old dog, he knew that, and deep down he knew it was only a matter of time, but it didn't make it any easier when they lost him. He and Billy were devastated.

'Ed would've loved this,' he said to Billy as they walked along.

'Yeah. He always came to the market with us, didn't he?'

'He'd definitely have loved those pies over there,' said Doc. She sniffed the air. 'Smells great.'

'He'd have eaten two of them in one go,' Terri said.

'Let's get some.' Gran set off for the pie stall. 'Mrs Scott's pies are delicious. Come on, we'll all have one. Duke? Meatball?'

'Count us in,' Meatball said. 'Thanks, Mrs Makepeace.'

They stomped across the mud and sodden hessian sacks to stand beneath the awning. At least here there was some shelter. The heavy rain of the last two weeks had reduced the field to a bog.

Joseph dipped a hand into his pocket. 'Here, kids,' he said and then stopped as he saw Spike's face.

'I'm fourteen, Mr Price,' Spike said. 'We all are. Even Bill's twelve.'

Joseph took a breath. 'My apologies, everyone,' he said. 'I was just going to ask if you'd like to go on the machines in the marquee, while your Gran and I do some Christmas shopping.'

'Yeah, brilliant!' Billy yelled.

'Come and find us in about an hour,' said Gran. 'We might have a cup of tea as well.' She blew on her hands. 'Looks like you were right about the snow, Joseph.'

Joseph offered his arm. 'I usually am.'

Spike and the others laughed as they watched them walk off. Gran and Mr Price were the closest of friends, but behaved like an old married couple.

'Yes!'

Billy yelled out, as coins pumped rhythmically into the metal tray. 'I've done it! I've got the jackpot!'

He bent down and began scooping up the coins into a cup.

'Not now, you ain't,' growled a voice beside him. 'Out of the way, runt.'

Brett Tyler gave Billy a push that sent him flying.

'Oh yes, he has.'

5

Brett turned. Spike stood behind him, his face tight with anger. Behind him stood Duke and Meatball, Terri and Doc.

'Clear off, Tyler, if you know what's good for you,' Terri said.

Brett pulled a face. 'Why? What are you going to do, girly? Oh, look at me, I'm scared.'

'You ought to be,' said Meatball.

'Huh!'

With a derisory snort, Brett pushed through and stalked off.

Still seething, Spike watched him go. One day, he thought. One day.

'You all right, Bill?'

Billy shook himself loose from Doc's grip. 'Course I'm all right!'

Duke looked down at the coins in the metal tray. 'You won the jackpot, Bill? You jammy …'

'I hate Brett Tyler,' Billy said. 'I wish Ed was here, he'd have had him.'

Spike nodded sadly. 'I wish he was here, too. It's not the same without him.'

'He'll be watching,' Terri said. 'He can probably smell the pies from up there.'

'Where?' Duke asked.

Terri shrugged. 'I don't know.' She looked at Spike. 'Let's talk about something else. He wouldn't want you to be sad, would he?' She gave a slight glance in Billy's direction.

Spike met her gaze. She was right. She usually was. He and Terri had always been close and he trusted her judgement.

'Yeah,' he said, in a lighter tone. 'Yeah, you're right. Especially as Bill's just offered to buy us all doughnuts.'

'*Eh?*'

Laughing, they walked out of the marquee and across to the doughnut stall. The hot doughnuts were soft, fluffy and deliciously sweet.

'We'd better think about finding your gran and Mr Price,' Duke said, glancing at his watch. 'It's been about an hour.'

'Good idea,' said Meatball. 'Mr Price might think we're having a ride on the teacups.'

'You'd never fit in a teacup,' Doc said, laughing. 'You wouldn't even get your bum in it.'

'Just because we could fit the whole of you into a teacup,' he said.

Doc stuck out her chin. 'So? That might come in handy one day.'

'Yeah, you never know,' Spike said. 'We might ...'

He paused, staring into the distance.

'What is it?'

'I don't know, Bill, it's just ... well, I could've sworn ...'

'What?'

Spike looked back at them. 'A guy I just saw in the distance over there. I'd swear it was Gullivan.'

'*Gullivan*?'

'It can't have been,' Duke said. 'He's gone. Mr Price said. His house is all closed up. No-one's seen him.'

'Yeah, I know, but ...'

'It can't have been Gullivan,' said Meatball. 'He's long gone.'

'It was probably just someone that looks like him,' said Doc.

'Yeah ... yeah, probably.' Spike looked across at Terri. Her eyes were searching his, as though she knew what he was thinking, which wouldn't really have surprised him. She had an empathy like that with other people and animals. Sometimes, it was almost as if she knew what they were thinking, and her gift seemed to have grown stronger this last year.

And if she could read his thoughts, she'd know exactly what those thoughts were. Gullivan ... could that man in the distance really have been him? If it was, he was the last person they wanted to see. Cornelius Gullivan was Gran's neighbour, an evil, cold, disgusting man who thought nothing of shooting anything that ventured onto his land. It didn't seem a year since they'd last seen him. Could he really be back?

'There they are!'

Duke's voice cut into his thoughts.

Spike looked up. Gran and Mr Price were walking towards them.

'You all ready?' Gran asked.

'Yes, thanks, Gran.'

'Then I thought we might make a move home,' she said. 'It's getting really quite cold now, isn't it? Did you win anything?'

'Billy won the jackpot,' Terri said. 'And a push in the back from Tyler.'

Gran frowned. 'Not again,' she said. 'You all right, love?'

Billy nodded. 'Course,' he said, defiantly. 'It's only Tyler.'

Mr Price stopped to shuffle several bags of shopping. 'Does that foul boy ever stop making trouble?'

Duke and Meatball walked across to help him with the bags.

'Thanks, lads. Come on, let's get back on the bus. I can't feel my feet.'

'See you at *school*, Collins.'

The shout drifted on the increasing wind. On the steps of the old bus, Billy turned.

'Shut up, Tyler,' he shouted.

'Ignore that loser,' Duke murmured. 'He's not worth it.'

Spike nodded. 'I know.'

And deep down, he did know, Brett Tyler wasn't worth it, but he still hated him.

'Course, that doesn't mean I wouldn't like to wipe that smug grin off his face,' Meatball growled as he stepped on the bus.

Duke looked back over his shoulder. 'Yeah,' he said. 'And me.'

'Everybody ready?'

Joseph Price glanced over his shoulder, then turned and slipped the bus into gear. Slowly, it moved off.

Shaking and rattling, the old bus climbed the rough pitted stone road. Through the window, Terri watched Brett Tyler lean slowly down and scoop something into his hand. Drawing back his arm, he took aim at the bus, but before he could throw the handful of muck, his feet slipped from under him and he wobbled forwards.

With a loud shriek, he overbalanced completely and plunged face first into the filth. For a moment, he lay squirming in the dirt, and then unsteadily, he pushed himself up on one elbow. Disgusting, slimy mess dripped from his face in huge globs. Desperately, he tried to right himself but his knee slid away, sending him back onto the ground, hitting the mud with a loud splat.

On board the bus, Terri watched, squealing with delight. The others pressed against the windows, shouting and cheering.

'Gran! Mr Price!'

Gran turned to look. 'What ... oh my *goodness* ...'

Joseph stopped the bus and turned around in his seat. 'What on earth's the matter?'

Billy was almost jumping up and down. 'Look, it's Tyler! It's Tyler! He's face down in the muck!'

Doc scrambled about in her pocket for her phone. 'I've got to get a picture of this,' she squealed. 'I've got to get a picture of it for school!'

Spike watched Brett squirm in the mud, trying desperately to wipe it from his face.

'Well, I never,' Gran said. She cleared her throat, and then turned to look at Joseph Price. 'What d'you make of that, Joseph?'

Giving her a quick smile, Joseph glanced over her shoulder and out through the window. With a slight cough, he said, 'Well, I never. That boy should really take more care. How very, very unfortunate.'

Everyone was still laughing about Brett Tyler on the drive home. Doc had managed to take several photos of him as they left, and they'd have plenty to show around school. Of course, everyone knew Brett would be making plans to get his own back, but they didn't care. It had been worth it.

As the bus turned into the top of the long road to the village, a few light flakes of snow were drifting on the air. Mr Price had been right, here it was, the first snow of the winter.

By the time they reached the village square, it was snowing in earnest. Huge, fluffy flakes littered the sky, falling clumsily to the ground in a heap as though someone had unzipped the clouds.

Wrapped in his own thoughts, Spike stared out of the window.

'You think it was him, don't you?'

He turned to see Terri looking at him.

'Maybe,' he said, and then turned away. He didn't want Terri guessing his next thoughts, though she probably had a fair idea. If the figure he saw *was* Gullivan, it could only mean trouble.

CHAPTER TWO

The following day, they were sitting in the basement of Meatball's home.

Spike looked around. Meatball had this whole basement as a den and it was fantastic. Warm, cosy, and quiet, save for the background hum of electrical equipment, it was home to his collection of computers and other technology.

Meatball was obsessed with technology. Whenever anything new came out, he would do odd jobs and chores and save every penny from Christmas and birthdays until he could afford to buy it, and then things would go very quiet for a while until he'd mastered it.

Terri glanced down at the rug. It was where Meatball's cat could be found whenever he was at home. Today it was empty.

'No Gus today then?' she asked.

Meatball shook his head. 'No, he's at work with Dad today.'

'I swear he gets bigger every time I see him,' she said.

Gus was an enormous Maine Coon cat, who'd adopted Meatball and his family.

It was Meatball's dad who'd discovered a fluffy ginger kitten fast asleep in the back of his car when he arrived home from work one day. It had been very hot and the car parked with the windows down, and at some point, Gus had obviously jumped in the back and made himself at home.

The usual enquiries had been made, but no one had come forward to claim him, so he'd stayed, and every morning, he went to work with Meatball's dad at the Stately Home, where Gus was now something of a celebrity.

Probably fast asleep on his usual chair, Spike thought, or striding around the Stately Home to meet the visitors. He was the right size to be Meatball's cat, broad shouldered, and muscled, just like him.

'Gus is a brilliant cat,' said Duke, striding across to the biscuit tin. 'I love the fact he takes up all the sofa when he sits on it.'

'Bit like you,' Doc muttered.

'I can't help it,' Duke said, wrenching the lid off the biscuit tin. 'My legs keep growing. Here, you had all the biscuits again, Meatball?'

'Might've done,' said Meatball. 'Anyway, it was your turn to bring the biscuits.'

Duke pulled a face. 'Oh yeah, I forgot.'

'You can't expect him to remember biscuits when he's got all that royal stuff to do,' said Terri, smirking.

Spike laughed. As long as they'd known him, Duke had been convinced he had royal blood. His mum and dad said the whole idea was ludicrous, but he believed it anyway.

Meatball's voice cut into his thoughts. 'No worries,' he said, suddenly. 'Mum's left us some bread for toast.'

He grabbed half a loaf off the cabinet and threw it to Duke. 'Here, hold this. I'll get the forks.'

He pulled two large toasting forks from the drawer. Minutes later, the bread was being toasted carefully over the glowing coals of the fire by Duke and Doc.

'I can't wait,' Doc cried, as the bread began to brown.

'Me, neither,' said Terri, fixing her eyes on the butter. 'I'm starving.'

Doc flipped the toast over. 'No, I mean Tyler, face down in all that gunge. I can't wait to show it round school.'

In a chair next to her, Spike smiled to himself. He was already thinking of the satisfaction he was going to feel showing that particular photograph around the school.

'We should run off loads,' yelled Billy. 'Put them up all over the school.'

'Reckon one very large one will do the trick,' Duke said. 'We can always run some more off.' He looked across at Spike. 'A nice big colour photo, eh?'

Spike grinned.

Sliding another slice of toast onto the table, Doc reloaded the fork. 'Better wait and see how they come out first. Hopefully they're all right. I took them a bit quick.'

'Wait's over,' said Meatball.

He got up as a large glossy photo slid into the printer tray. 'Oh, *yes!* Look at this!'

Wiping buttery hands on his sweater, he leaned over and carefully lifted out the photo. A deep chuckle rumbled in his throat. 'Oh, look at this, guys. You've got to see it!'

They gathered round. In the middle of the table a large photo glistened in the firelight, and there he was in all his glory. Brett Tyler, spread flat in the glutinous gloop, face, legs, and arms dripping with disgusting muck.

The basement erupted into howls and screeches of laughter.

Billy's voice rose to a squeal. 'It's the bog man we saw in that film the other week!'

'That is … brilliant,' Duke said.

Spike nodded in agreement. 'Got him,' he said. 'Nice one.'

Terri sighed. 'It's perfect,' she said.

Picking up the photo, Duke took a closer look at it.

'Oh look, he's got his little hat dirty,' he wailed. 'That's the best laugh I've had for ages. Here, hold on a minute …'

The smile dropped from his face. 'What on earth's that? I don't remember that.'

He laid the photo back on the table as the others looked on.

'What?'

Duke pointed at the photo. '*That*,' he said. 'There, look, over on that notice board thing, at the back. What is it?'

They stared at the photograph. In the middle of a large notice board at the entrance to the fair, a sign had appeared. It was a ring with three segments. Slowly, it started to expand. A tiny dot of purple sprang from the centre and spread outward to colour the whole sign, which then began to pulse. Terri gasped. 'What's happening? That can't be happening, it's a photo, not a video. How can something be moving in a photo?'

'That's not possible,' said Billy, shaking his head slowly. 'It's not possible. Is it?'

'Course not,' Spike snapped. 'There's something weird going on.'

As they watched, the sign continued to expand, growing larger and larger until, with one enormous throb of purple, it exploded in a shower of sparks and disappeared.

'It's gone!' Terri's eyes opened wide. 'Where'd it go?'

Meatball sat down, heavily. 'It was definitely there, I saw it.'

'We *all* saw it,' Duke said.

Spike put a hand on his head. 'D'you know, I've seen that somewhere before. That sign. I know I have.'

'It's the sign for radiation,' Doc said, quietly. 'That's what it is. They use that sign wherever there's any danger of radioactivity. But don't ask me what it was doing there or where it's gone.' She peered at the photo. 'There's nothing, not even a mark. Just a brick wall.'

'I suppose … I suppose we did see it. Did we?' Terri looked over Doc's shoulder at the photo. 'It wasn't a trick of the light, was it?'

Her voice trailed away.

'I definitely saw it,' said Billy.

'Oh, come on. We all saw it,' Duke said again. 'A purple radiation sign. It was definitely there.'

An eerie silence descended on the basement as each of them considered the pulsing sign, and tried to explain the unexplainable.

Duke stood up and said what they were all thinking. Picking up the photo, he examined it carefully, then in a clear, calm voice he said, 'Well, like I said, it was definitely there, a radiation sign, just long enough for us all to see it. Next thing we know, it's gone. Disappeared. The worrying thing is as well ... it was purple, and we all know what happened last time.'

A chill spread across Spike's back. How could he forget? When Joseph Price had suddenly disappeared the year before, he'd known instinctively that Gullivan had something to do with it, and it was then they'd followed him down to the bridge that spanned the river, and discovered he was using a time portal to travel back to prehistoric times, amassing a fortune in diamonds on the way. And it was there, in that strange land, they'd met and helped their new friends to leave Earth before an asteroid struck.

Gullivan hadn't been seen by any of them since. It's strange, Spike thought. Somehow, it seems like yesterday and years ago, all at the same time. Trauma does that, Doc had said. It's just one of the tricks your mind plays when something major happens.

'The way I see it,' Duke continued. 'That purple radiation sign can only mean one thing ...'

'It was meant for us,' Meatball interrupted, soberly. 'That's what you're going to say, isn't it? We were the only ones supposed to see it. Us, and only us. But what does it mean?'

CHAPTER THREE

In the lonely, barren surroundings of his new home in Roman Britain, Cornelius Gullivan looked around, remembering.

He'd been here almost a year now. It didn't seem possible; a whole year since he'd burst back through the time portal running for his life.

He'd only just made it, too. A second or two later and Molly McKendrick's bullets might not have missed. The thought sent a chill down his spine. Without the time portal, he'd have been a goner.

Gullivan thought about Molly McKendrick. She was not a nice person to know. Molly and her husband, Toby, were evil, and he had no desire to meet either of them ever again.

Toby was in prison now of course, but Gullivan had helped to put him there, and Molly was not the type to forgive or forget.

'Still,' he said. 'What can she do? She can hardly hurt me here, can she? I'm on the other side of a time portal she knows nothing about.'

He lit a cigarette and allowed himself a smile. The time portal. One way and another, it had come in very handy. If he hadn't spotted Joseph Price using it, he'd never have known about the world beyond, a prehistoric world with caves full of diamonds just ripe for the taking.

Unfortunately, there was also a race of weird-looking aliens who got in the way and he'd had to kill two of them. Just like those brats from the village. He'd like to kill them as well, always poking their noses in.

Still, who cared about any of them. They couldn't touch him here.

And neither could Molly McKendrick. He grinned. Her face must've been a picture. There she was, trying to gun him down and he'd simply disappeared into thin air. Vanished. He almost wished he'd been there to see it.

But luckily, he wasn't.

Of course, when he'd rushed through the time portal, he hadn't expected to end up here. He'd been expecting a cave, with tropical heat and dinosaurs, millions of years in the past. But something had gone wrong with the portal. Running for his life from Molly McKendrick, he'd stumbled through, tripped and landed, not in the world of dinosaurs, but in a large open field. And right in front of him, stood six olive-skinned men, broad and muscular and armed to the teeth with swords and spears.

Gullivan had recognised them quickly enough. Roman Legionaries.

Somehow, heart throbbing in his chest, he'd staggered to his feet, vaguely aware they were moving nearer, the lethal points of their spears now only a short distance from his face. He remembered the look in their dark eyes and the movement of their uniform.

Frantically, he'd raised the shotgun already sitting at his shoulder, but still, they kept coming.

He fired twice and the four still standing turned and ran for their lives.

Fishing in his pockets for more cartridges, he reloaded and lifted it to his shoulder, but when he looked up they had vanished without trace.

Gullivan's knees had given way then. Trembling with fear and exhaustion, he'd dropped to the ground, head reeling.

A new noise had made him look up. New figures, completely different people, were now coming toward him out of the long grass.

He remembered them, too, with very little effort. He'd thought at first he'd walked in on some sort of performance, one of those re-enactment things, especially as the new figures seemed to be wearing trousers. Long-haired and bearded, these men were dressed in brightly coloured tunics and armed with ferocious spears.

Staring at them, heart pounding, Gullivan's skin had pricked with sweat.

Time itself had seemed to slow.

He'd held the shotgun in his hand, gripping it tightly and knowing it would be useless against so many.

For a long moment he'd stared, disbelieving. Then his survival instinct had kicked in, and leaping to his feet, he'd turned on his heels and run back through the portal.

Bursting through on the other side, there he was again, standing back on the bridge in the twenty-first century. It was still the same on this side of the bridge, yet a different place on the other side. How was that possible?

He glanced up. There in front of him stood Molly McKendrick, gun still in her hand, and that huge lump of a sidekick of hers, both now staring at him, pale with shock, as Gullivan reappeared out of nowhere.

Mechanically, Molly had raised the gun still in her hand and pointed it directly at Gullivan's head.

No use … it was no use …

Whimpering, Gullivan had turned again, running back through to Roman Britain, and found himself back in the long green grass, with the natives staring, gasping and muttering.

A miracle had happened then. In one last frantic gesture, he raised his gun and fired into the air … and the natives had dropped to their knees and bowed down before him.

They'd watched this man vanish and then reappear, heard the ear-splitting noise and seen the killing power of the long stick he carried.

This man was a God.

Now, a year later, those same people were standing outside the little temple they'd built, without the faintest idea it was right over a time portal. He could come and go as he pleased and to them it was just one more miracle.

Pathetic fools, he thought. Ignorant, superstitious fools.

But useful for the time being. At the moment, they'd do anything Gullivan asked of them, anything he could draw an image of in the dark earth, and that was proving very useful indeed, particularly when he clapped eyes on the little trinkets they were bringing him as gifts.

Maybe their own work, maybe stolen from their foreign invaders, but who gave a damn. As long as those trinkets shone with gold and precious jewels, they were all right in his book.

In the corner, he stared down at the stash of gold artefacts he'd already collected, and selected an exquisite gold figure studded with gems. He stroked the surface gently with his fingers.

'Time for a trip home to the twenty-first Century, I think,' he said. 'Stash you and all the other treasures under the floorboards. I know a couple of guys who'll be very interested and don't ask questions.'

He'd waited many weeks before returning home again and the first time, he'd stepped through onto the bridge with shotgun raised, ready to fire. But time, it seemed, had moved on in the twenty-first century as well, and Molly McKendrick was gone.

Thank God.

With any luck he'd never see her again, or that vicious thug of hers, but the fact remained that every time he went back to the present day, he was taking a risk. He hadn't seen them, either by the portal or near his home, but there was always that chance.

One thing he knew for sure. Molly McKendrick wouldn't rest until he was dead.

Then there was his other problem. The local natives: the indigenous people here in Roman Britain. How long would it be, he wondered, before they turned against him?

Gullivan stood for a second or two thinking about home in the twenty-first century and all its luxuries, and he heaved a long sigh.

He'd love to go back for good, but it was going to be risky. The McKendricks weren't the sort to forget, and their informers were everywhere.

But it was either that or face the inevitable moment the people here in Roman Britain decided they too, had had enough of him.

CHAPTER FOUR

In the kitchen of Yew Tree Cottage, Billy sat finishing the last of his cereal.

'Well,' he said, vaguely, 'it doesn't look as though anything's going to happen. Duke told us to look out for things, but nothing's happened.'

Beside him, Spike crunched on a burnt piece of toast. 'We don't know that it's going to,' he said, 'but that business with the photo was odd. And Duke's right, we can't explain it, so it's worth keeping our eyes open for anything else. And it's only been two weeks since we saw it.'

Billy jabbed at a malted square with his spoon. 'S'pose. Still, we start the Christmas holidays today.' He broke off to clench his fists with pleasure. 'Yay!'

At last, thought Spike, at last I might get a bit of peace.

The photo had gone down a storm at school, and Brett Tyler had neither forgiven nor forgotten. At least now, he thought, with any luck, I won't have to see him for nearly three weeks.

Down the hallway, the doorbell rang out. Billy dropped his spoon with a clatter, leaped to his feet, and threw open the kitchen door to run down the hall.

Spike glanced down the hall after him. Through the glass of the front door, he saw the shadow of a tall figure. It reminded him of the day, almost a year before, when the shadow at the door had been Cornelius Gullivan. On that day, Gullivan had been carrying his shotgun and it had taken all Spike's strength to hold back dear old Ed.

A terrible thought washed over him. What if the figure he'd seen was him and he was back? What if that shadow at the door was him again?

With a sudden jolt, Spike leaped from his chair and dashed after them.

The door opened. With relief, he saw the visitor was Frank, the postman.

'Hello, Frank.'

'Morning!'

Frank stood on the doorstep, coated with snow. 'What a day.'

He handed them a bunch of letters and cards. 'Here you go, lads, give these to your gran. Take care now, this snow's pretty bad. Mind you, don't suppose you care much now the Christmas holidays are here, eh? Cheerio!'

He trudged slowly off down the path, and Spike shut the door. 'That reminds me, Bill,' he said, 'we'd better get a move on. This snow's going to slow us right down. I'll tell Gran we're going.'

He gave the cards a quick glance, and one of them suddenly caught his attention.

'Hello,' he said. 'There's one here for us.'

Slipping a finger under the flap, he tore it open and looked at the card. It was a picture of a hillside dressed in snow with sparkling Christmas trees. A wreath of holly and ivy wound its way around the edge.

Spike stared at it for a moment, and then opened it and read the verse aloud.

'*The holly and the ivy, when they are both full grown. This should put you on the right track, if you've got tunnel vision.*'

'Eh?' he said. 'What's that all about?'

They both frowned.

'Sounds a bit weird,' said Billy. 'Who's it from?'

Spike studied the card, examining its every detail from front to back. 'Don't know … there's nothing on it.' He checked the envelope. 'It's definitely addressed to us, Bill. Wait a minute though, it's got no stamp or postmark, so how did Frank get it?'

'Maybe someone gave it to him.'

Spike shook his head, doubtfully. 'No. He'd have said something.'

'Hey, look!'

Billy grabbed the envelope and thrust it near Spike's face. 'It's purple, the envelope's purple! It's another thing, it's got to be. We have to tell the others.'

Spike nodded, thoughtfully. 'Maybe … yeah, you might be right, Bill, it could be something. We'll mention it at the meeting. Talking of which, let's get going, we're due at Meatball's in fifteen minutes.'

As he and Billy trudged through the snow down the lane, he gave thanks it had only been Frank at the door.

If it had been Gullivan, he wasn't sure what he'd have done. How he hated him. Everything that evil man touched seemed to shrivel and die. It was as if his mere presence drew all the life out of things, leaving them broken and colourless.

Walking along, he looked out across the fields. In the distance, Gullivan's land was just visible: white and barren. Pulling his scarf tighter about his neck, he prayed silently that Gullivan would never return.

They carried on further down the lane and saw Terri walking down the path to her front gate, well wrapped and booted against the cold.

'All right, Terri?'

'Yes.' She held a carrier bag in her hand. 'Biscuits,' she said, in answer to their looks. 'Mum said I could bring some. Make a change from eating all Meatball's stuff. Don't suppose you thought to bring any?'

They shook their heads.

'What sort of biscuits?'

'I don't know, Billy. Round ones. Don't ask me, I just grabbed them out of the cupboard.'

Stomping slowly on through the snow, they turned up the street through the village and on to Meatball's home.

By the time they arrived, Duke and Doc were already there and the kettle was boiling.

Terri held up the carrier bag. 'Mum sent some biscuits,' she said.

'Great.' Meatball prised himself out of a sofa and walked across to test the biscuits. 'What sort?'

'You're as bad as them,' said Terri, tutting. 'I don't know. Have a look.'

Spike gave Terri a sideways glance. It wasn't like her to snap like that. Maybe something was worrying her. Maybe that baby brother of hers had been screaming again.

Over on the cabinet the kettle started to whistle. Doc made six cups of hot chocolate and Meatball passed them around.

'Right.'

Duke waited until everyone had finished dunking biscuits and then stood up to take charge of the meeting the way he always did, as though he truly believed he had royal blood.

Slowly, he ran a hand through his blond hair and declared the meeting open. 'First,' he said, solemnly. 'I think we should all take a moment to remember.'

The others stopped slurping chocolate and stared at him.

Slowly, Duke raised his head to meet their gaze, then suddenly yelled, 'Brett Tyler's face when he saw that *photo!*'

'Yeah!' Meatball's arm shot into the air and nearly sent the small rickety table flying.

'Yay!' cried Billy.

Laughter rang around the room.

'His face was a picture,' Spike said.

'Literally,' Doc squealed.

Terri wiped a tear from her eye and then slowly stopped laughing. 'Only thing that bothers me,' she said, 'is he'll be determined to get us back, him and those mates of his. Especially you, Spike.'

He shrugged. 'Forget it. I'll be ready for him.'

Terri took a deep breath and leaned across to whisper. 'Not just about you, though, is it?'

Spike glanced at her. He knew what she meant. Brett Tyler wouldn't hesitate to make life difficult for Billy if it suited him.

'Don't worry,' he whispered. 'I've got his back.'

Terri rolled her eyes. 'Like you're going to be there all the time.' She broke off as Billy looked round.

'Who?' he asked.

Spike smiled at him. 'Nothing, mate.' He watched Terri give a sharp sigh. She was in a bad mood today. He felt even more certain that something was worrying her. Ok, the sign they'd seen in the photo could be the start of something, maybe even something dangerous, but it was a bit early to start worrying, wasn't it? Instinctively, he knew there was something else: something Terri hadn't mentioned yet.

'Right,' Duke said, 'back to business. You know I said we should all look out for anything weird? Well, something else has happened. I don't think it's connected with the sign we saw in that photo, I can't really see how it can be, but ...'

'What is it?' Doc asked.

Duke looked across at Meatball. 'Tell them what you told me earlier.'

'Well,' said Meatball, 'I know this is going to sound odd, but this morning I saw someone walking away from me.'

Spike looked at him, curiously. 'What d'you mean?'

'At home, you mean?' Doc asked. 'Your mum was walking away from you?'

Meatball shook his head. 'No. Though it was a woman.'

'Right.'

'A woman who was with you at breakfast,' said Terri.

'No. She wasn't actually there.'

Spike frowned at him. 'So how could you see her if she wasn't there?'

'Ah, I get it. You mean you had one of your dreams again,' Terri said.

'No, that's the thing, I was wide awake,' said Meatball. 'I was sitting there, having breakfast and I suddenly saw a picture, a sort of image right in front of me. There was a woman.'

'Did you recognise her?'

25

'No, but then like I said, she was walking away, so I could only see the back of her.'

He paused, staring straight ahead for a moment or two, obviously trying to recapture the image. 'But the funny thing is, she did feel kind of familiar.'

'A back view of someone can be just as familiar and recognisable as a front view,' Doc said. 'But you can't think who she was?'

Again, Meatball shook his head, vaguely. 'No.'

'What was she doing?' asked Terri. 'Apart from walking, I mean.'

Billy leaned in a bit closer. 'What was she wearing?'

A light came on in Meatball's eyes. 'That's a point, Bill, she was wearing some sort of uniform. Least, I think she was. It's hard to know.' He drifted again in a world of his own thoughts. 'And there was something else. Her legs …'

'What about her legs?'

Meatball screwed up his face. 'That's the problem, I don't really know. You know how sometimes you notice something that seems odd but you can't think what it is?'

Spike nodded. 'So where did she go?'

'I don't know that, either. The picture faded after, but she was definitely walking away from me. Quite quickly too.' He suddenly snapped his fingers. 'Hang on. A door. There was a door!'

'What sort of a door?'

Meatball slumped back in his chair. 'It's gone,' he said.

'It's definitely weird,' said Duke. 'And we've got to watch out for odd stuff at the moment, but I can't see what it's got to do with anything. Especially that sign we saw.'

'Nor me,' Spike murmured, thoughtfully, 'but we can't ignore anything. And as it happens, me and Bill have got something as well.'

Billy pulled the Christmas card from his pocket. 'We got this in this morning's post,' he said. 'It was in with all the rest.' He slid the card onto the table. 'It's got no stamp and no postmark, and it's addressed to us, but we don't get what's written inside.'

Doc picked it up and read it aloud.

'That's a funny sort of Christmas card,' Duke said. 'And there's no signature.'

Meatball nodded slowly. 'That's definitely weird. What's it mean?'

Spike shrugged.

'And look at the envelope,' said Billy. 'It's purple.'

Meatball picked up the envelope and turned it slowly over in his hands. 'Well, I suppose cards do have purple envelopes,' he said. 'But I think you're right, Bill, that could mean something.'

'Could be coincidence, I suppose,' Spike said, 'but with everything else that's been happening ... I'll hang onto it, it might be important.' He took a deep breath. 'So, that's three things now.'

'Four.'

Terri's single word caught their attention.

'I didn't think about this when it happened,' she said. 'To be honest, I only realised after what it might mean. This morning I went to the shops to get some milk for Mum and on the way back I saw something.' She looked down at the floor, thinking. 'Least I think I did. It was pouring down with snow and I'm not really sure.' She looked anxious. 'I *think* I saw a purple light in the sky, though I might've been wrong.'

Spike whirled around. 'A purple light? Are you sure, Terri?'

'Well, I think so. Like I said, it was snowing and it was way over in the distance in the other direction, not near the bridge.'

'Was it ... an arc?' Duke asked, slowly.

Terri shrugged. 'I don't know, I only saw a faint glimmer, like something had been there, but it was fading.'

A purple arc in the sky. The previous year a purple arc had led them to a time portal, danger, and an experience they would never forget.

'Could be a time portal,' Billy breathed. 'D'you think that means there's one open again?'

'We don't know that, Bill,' Duke said, cautiously. 'We don't even know for sure if you saw it, Terri, but if you did, it's what else it might mean that's worrying. It's one thing for a time portal somewhere to be open, but if you did see that flash …'

'Exactly.' Doc nodded. 'Someone's using it.'

CHAPTER FIVE

By the time Spike, Billy, and their friends reached the top of the hill, they were already shivering, but were determined to try to search the house and see if there were any signs of Gullivan's return.

There had to be a reason for that light in the sky. Somewhere a time portal was in use and he was the obvious suspect.

Not that they wanted to meet him, he was revolting. Most of the time, he looked as if he hadn't washed in weeks, and he lived like an absolute pig. If he'd been back, there'd be some sign all right.

They carried on, trudging laboriously through the snow until they reached the dense hedge that encircled his land.

Spike looked at it. Twelve feet high and studded with vicious spines, the hedge was almost impossible to get through. It stood between them and Gullivan's land like a solid wall. There was only one way of getting through unscathed and now it rose up before them, its bleak snow-covered arms reaching out across the landscape.

Solomon.

Solomon was an ancient oak tree on the edge of Gullivan's land. Hundreds of years old, it had been struck by lightning many years before and was now just a blackened trunk, but inside it was hollow and this was their way into Gullivan's field, a secret way discovered by Spike.

Approaching the huge corrugated trunk, they carefully swept the snow away, then sliding their fingers beneath a loose panel, lifted it clear, and stepped into the eerie gloom of the empty trunk. Past crumbling walls and scurrying insects, they pushed their way through to the panel on the opposite side.

The field stretched away into the distance: still and bitterly cold, a dead space wrapped in a shroud of snow.

'Can't see anything,' Duke said, screwing up his eyes. He stepped outside, the frozen surface cracking noisily beneath his boots.

Spike stepped out behind him. 'That doesn't mean anything. You know how he creeps about. He could be anywhere.'

'If he's back,' said Terri. 'We don't even know he is.'

'It's really quiet,' said Billy. He glanced up at the trees, still and silent, muffled by snow. There was no sign of the crows that usually cawed at the slightest interruption. 'Nothing's moving.'

'He could've shot everything,' Meatball said. 'You know what he's like. Might be a sign.'

Doc pulled her collar tightly around her neck. 'Let's get a bit nearer the house. If he is about, there'll be some sign he's around. Got to be.'

As they trudged along, Terri peered ahead. 'Surely there'd be a light or something,' she said. 'He's got to have light, hasn't he?' She looked up at the oppressive stone-grey sky. 'It's going to be dark soon. He's got to have some light. We'll see it, if there's a candle or something. We'll spot that easily.'

Closer to the house, everything was in darkness. If Gullivan was back, he was taking great care not to show it.

'Looks deserted,' Doc said. 'Course, he might just be playing it safe, in case those gangsters are still around.'

Spike thought about the gangsters. It was the only name they had for the couple that had mysteriously appeared in the village the previous year. Billy had been the first to spot them. The man was large, with a thick-neck, a square head and greying hair. He wore a heavy, fur-collared coat and black leather gloves. With him was a tall, skinny woman who was clearly in charge. She had glossy black hair and red lips and was dressed in ridiculous clothes and shoes.

Billy had watched them wander around, stopping passers-by to ask questions and showing shopkeepers a photograph. Once he had managed to glance at it and realise these strangers were looking for Cornelius Gullivan, he'd wasted no time telling Spike and the others.

'I reckon the gangsters are long gone,' said Meatball. 'They were hanging about in the village for a bit last year after he disappeared, but they soon gave up and we haven't seen them since.'

Setting off along the hedge, they kept their backs to the long thorns lurking beneath the surface of the snow. The light was slowly fading; fresh flakes were falling in fits and starts.

Clouds of warm breath hung in the air as they made their way across the field and into the hay barn, then swiftly on to the side of the house.

It looked empty, still and eerily silent.

Creeping along the wall, Duke peered into one of the lower windows through a thick film of grime.

'Hard to see anything much,' he said.

Spike moved closer to the next window and brushed aside the snow collected on the narrow ridge.

'Pigs like him don't clean windows,' he murmured. 'He probably doesn't want anyone to see inside anyway.'

He glanced around. 'We need to get in. Look, you lot wait here and I'll try the coal cellar.'

It wasn't the first time they'd used the coal cellar to get into Gullivan's house, but it was dirty and dangerous.

'I'll come with you,' Duke said. 'Better if there's two of us, just in case.'

'Good idea,' said Meatball. He stamped his feet in a feeble attempt to warm his toes. 'But be quick, he may be around and it's freezing out here. We'll wait outside and keep a look out. If you're not out in a few minutes, we'll come in to look for you.'

Billy started forward. 'I'll come in with you.'

Spike shook his head. 'No, Bill. You stay here with Meatball and the others.'

'But I helped last time. I'm not a kid.'

'It's nothing to do with that, Bill,' said Meatball, gripping his arm. 'But you're brighter than Duke and Spike, and I might need your brains.'

Billy rolled his eyes. 'Yeah, all right.'

The door of the coal cellar was still slightly ajar, as they'd left it on their last visit, and the bitter wind had blown snow in through the opening, across the floor and halfway up the staircase.

Once inside, Duke switched on a torch and shone the bright beam up the stairs and onto the door above.

'Watch the bottom of the door with that light!'

Whipping the torchlight to the opposite wall, Duke cursed beneath his breath. 'Sorry. Didn't think.'

They stood silently in the gloom for a few moments, listening. There was no sound.

Cautiously, they made their way a little closer to the door. 'I don't reckon he's here.'

'Doesn't sound like it,' Duke hissed, 'but you never know with him. You know what he's like, he could be waiting.'

A piece of coal hidden in the snow suddenly crunched beneath Spike's boot, the noise reverberating around the tomb-like conditions of the cellar. He held his breath. Duke pulled his head down into the thick collar of his coat, stared across at Spike, and waited. Still no sound.

Duke nodded toward the door. 'We're going to have to chance it.'

Together they climbed the few steps to the door. Stretching out a hand, Spike gripped the brass handle and felt it spring back from his grasp. He pulled off his glove, and then, taking a firm hold on the handle, turned until the lock eased open.

Signalling to Duke to move forward, he swung the door gently outwards, peered out, and then looked up and down the hallway, listening for the slightest sound.

He glanced at Duke, who nodded, and then they left the cellar and stepped out.

In the hallway, it was still and quiet, the air stale, the surfaces shrouded beneath a thick veil of dust. Spike felt a nudge in his ribs and looked around to see Duke nodding toward the floor. There on the parquet flooring were clear signs that the dust had been disturbed.

They looked across to the stairs. In places the bannisters were streaked clean.

'He's been here,' Duke mouthed.

Spike took a long sniff. 'Somebody has.' He nodded. 'Smells like him.'

'Could it be the gangsters?'

He pulled a face. 'Let's hope not. Don't want to meet them either.'

Tiptoeing slowly across the hallway, he leaned around the door of the kitchen.

It was in an appalling state, as always. The putrid smell of tobacco smoke, alcohol and stale sweat hung on the air. On the table stood an empty plate and glass and beside them, a bowl overflowing with cigarette butts. The sink was filthy and the draining board was strewn with empty bottles.

From the doorway, Spike stared at it. There was no mistaking that particular stench. A mix of fear and hatred coursed through his body. 'He's back all right.'

Duke glanced over his shoulder. Gullivan could be anywhere and he couldn't be trusted. Something brushed across his leg and he jerked and let out a muffled croak.

'*Mouse*.' Spike's arm gripped his. 'It's only a mouse.' He looked about the dismal, smelly kitchen. 'I don't like the feel of this. Let's get out.'

'Well?'

Meatball answered his own question before either of them had the chance. 'He's back, isn't he? I can tell by the look on your face. Somehow he's found a way back.'

Duke nodded.

'You're sure?' Terri grasped Spike's arm. 'How d'you know it's him, did you see him? It could be some passing tramp.'

Spike looked at her. 'It's him, all right,' he growled. 'I'd know that putrid smell anywhere.'

'Oh hell, that's not good news,' Doc said. 'Let's go home. The snow's getting heavier, and it'll take us a while to cross the field. Come on, we can talk about everything when we get back.'

Inside Solomon, the air was almost suffocating, bitterly cold and steeped with the smell of mould and damp earth, but stepping through the doorway, they sighed with relief.

At the end of the line, Spike grasped the panel and slid it into place. Then, pulling his coat tightly around him, he followed the others through and out into the field.

Had Gullivan found a way back? Was it him that had been in the house, or could it just be a tramp taking shelter?

No, it was definitely his smell. No one else stank like that. But why now?

The gnawing wind whipped snowflakes into his face, and he pulled his hood tightly closed. He had an awful feeling this was only the beginning of something far more worrying. He stomped along through the snow, head down, thinking about everything. Somehow, Gullivan had found a way back to the present, and that meant he was using a time portal.

Spike's mind conjured up a picture of the time portal on the bridge over the river: the portal they'd used the year before. Gullivan couldn't be using that same one, or he'd have been back earlier, and someone would have noticed something.

And that portal wasn't exactly reliable anyway, especially since the electrical storm. But what about the arc of light Terri had seen? It wasn't near the river, she said, which meant there was another one. If only Ed was here. He'd soon sniff him out.

Shivering slightly, he suddenly wished old Ed was by his side, plodding through the snow, his scruffy grey mane littered with snowflakes. His heart ached. There were times when he missed Ed so much it hurt.

A deep *woof* shattered his thoughts like an explosion. Spike paused, rooted to the spot. Another bark followed, louder and nearer. How?

He looked up, peering frantically through the swirling snow. *Ed?* No. No ... this was ridiculous, it couldn't be.

At that moment, a large grey head and body came into view, bobbing and bouncing towards them on gangly legs, pounding the snow with huge paws.

Spike's throat went dry. '*Ed* ...?'

The huge Irish wolfhound bounded at them and launched himself at Spike, almost knocking him off his feet.

Tears welled in Spike's eyes as he sank his hands into the wiry coat.

'It isn't him.' Terri's voice was in his ear, soft but insistent. 'It isn't him.'

'I *know*,' he snapped. His voice softened. 'I know ... but he's great, isn't he?'

Billy threw his arms around the dog's neck. 'Where's he come from, Spike? Whose is he?'

They heard a faint call through the snow.

'Mason? Mason? Where are you, you stupid dog?'

'Over here!'

Meatball shouted into the distance and soon after, the figure of a man appeared out of the snow. 'Mason! You bad dog!'

The man stepped forward and attached a lead to the dog's collar. 'Sorry, kids,' he said. 'I keep trying to train him, but the wife spoils him and he gets away with blue murder. Hope he didn't hurt you?'

'Course not.'

'Nah, that's fine,' said Billy. 'We like dogs.'

'Yeah?' The man made some effort to get Mason to sit, but failed. 'Well, I'm not over keen myself. My wife's the one who wanted him. She saw a wolfhound when she was down here on a little trip last year and she took a fancy to it.

Five-minute wonder, I expect, like everything else. Anyway, sorry again. Come on, you mutt, let's get going.'

The man and his dog disappeared through the snow, and they continued on their way.

'I don't reckon he likes that dog,' Billy said, sulkily, 'the way he kept calling him names.'

'The dog doesn't like him much, either,' said Terri. 'He doesn't like him at all. He told me.'

CHAPTER SIX

The following morning, Duke stood in his bedroom peering closely at his face in the mirror. Not a thing. Zilch. Not even a prickle. His shoulders heaved in a huge sigh. Why? Why hadn't he got anything? Meatball had definite signs of a beard coming, even Spike had a bit of fuzz here and there and Duke was now a bit taller than both of them, so where was his beard? Delving into his bedside drawer, he retrieved the magnifying glass he kept for looking at spots, and squinted back at his chin in the mirror, looking again for any signs of stubble.

Several minutes searching later he threw the glass onto the bed and sat down. It wasn't fair, it wasn't *fair*.

Duke grasped an imaginary razor and dragged it across his chin. Soon, he thought, it had to be soon. Then he'd be doing this for real.

Looking up into the mirror, he closed his eyes and tried to imagine what he'd look like with a beard. It'd be real prickly at first, wouldn't it, like stroking a hedgehog. In the imaginary world behind his eyelids, Duke ran his fingers over the sharp spikes.

With a sudden jolt, he realised it wasn't his imagination; his chin really *was* covered in prickly hairs: thick hairs that dug into his fingers and scraped across his skin. Heart pounding in his throat, he slowly opened one eye, then the other, and with a loud yell of alarm, fell back onto his bed.

Aaagh! How had that happened? He had a *beard*! He had stubble! *Stubble!*

Duke dragged in a deep breath. He was imagining it, it wasn't *real*: it couldn't be.

He felt his chin again. It *was* real. There it was on his face: every stiff, thick, prickly hair of it. And it was getting thicker and longer.

'Stop it!' he yelled. 'Stop it! Stop growing!'

Gingerly, he touched it with a trembling hand. Was he dreaming or had it stopped?

He stared at it for a long moment until he decided it had stopped growing, although he still looked like that guy on EastEnders.

What *was* he going to do?

He took a long, deep breath and tried to still his heart. Ok, he thought. Calm. What would Doc say? What d'you do when something goes wrong? You analyse it. You look at it and work out what's happened.

He took another breath. Right. I've grown a beard. A beard! Aagh!

No … calm. This isn't normal, is it? But then, was anything normal these days? Look at last year. Aliens, dinosaurs, spaceships, time portals.

Duke closed his eyes. *Last year.*

The obvious washed over him in an enormous wave of relief. His special *skill*. Mr Price had said each of them would be getting special skills. He let that thought sit in his mind for a moment. Growing a beard was his special *skill*? Surely not. What use was that going to be?

He visualised them all, confronted by some appalling monster with enormous fangs. 'Don't panic, guys,' he could hear himself saying, 'I can grow a *beard*.'

So, we're looking down the barrel of Gullivan's shotgun? No problem, I can grow a beard.

The more Duke went over it, the more stupid it sounded. And what about the beard he'd just grown? What was he going to do about that? He hadn't even got a razor.

He let out a soft wail. How else was he going to get rid of this beard?

Hang on, he thought. If I can grow this lot by thinking about it, maybe I can get rid of it the same way. Nervously, he closed his eyes.

I do not want this beard, he said to himself. I want a smooth chin.

Slowly, he opened one eye. Then the other. The beard had gone! He clenched his fists. Yes!

He spent the next few minutes thinking, 'Beard ... no beard ... beard ... no beard,' watching as it appeared and disappeared at will. Next, he practised moving his ears, growing his nose and changing his hair.

An hour's practice later, and he could change his whole body into someone else entirely. Now *that*, he thought, is a special skill. Brilliant.

Tingling with excitement, he closed the door behind him and set off for Meatball's house. I can't wait to tell the others about this.

Perched in a small chair in Meatball's basement, Doc stretched her legs and yawned. 'I'm shattered,' she said. 'I couldn't sleep last night, thinking about stuff. Here, you remember that guy with the dog? D'you think it was Ed his wife saw last year?'

Meatball switched off his phone and slid it onto the cabinet. 'Probably,' he said.

'Same thought occurred to me,' Duke said.

'I bet it was,' said Billy, proudly. 'People always remember him. He was such a great looking dog.'

Spike nodded. 'Yeah, he was. Who were you on the phone to, Meatball?'

'Pizza place.'

'Pizza? What, this early?'

Meatball thumped his stomach. 'Didn't have any breakfast,' he said. 'Well, not much, only a couple of bowls of cereal.'

Spike laughed. Meatball was an eating machine.

'You're always hungry,' said Terri.

'Yep.'

'Sounds like a good idea to me,' Duke said.

Upstairs, the doorbell rang.

'Crikey, that's quick!'

'Probably last night's,' said Doc, looking queasy at the thought.

Before Meatball could move, Duke leaped to his feet. 'I'll go and have a look.'

They watched as he disappeared up the stairs.

'Duke must be starving,' said Terri. 'Hope he doesn't eat half of it.'

'He'd better not,' Meatball said. 'Or he's going out to get some more.'

Meatball turned his head with a jerk toward the stairs where a stocky figure in a coat and blue trousers was gingerly making his way down, holding several hot boxes.

'Yeah?'

The figure looked up. 'Sorry, he said it was all right.' He stared around at their blank faces. 'The fair haired, lanky guy,' he went on. 'He said it would be all right to bring them down. He said to say he's had to shoot off somewhere and to start without him.'

Meatball frowned but strode across to take the boxes. 'Thanks for that mate, that's nice of you. I'll take them.'

Spike stared at the pizza man, still frowning. 'Did he say where he was going?'

The man shook his head. 'Nah.'

'That's odd,' Doc said.

The man continued to wait.

Oh no, he wants a tip, thought Spike. He felt in his pocket. Twenty pence. Couldn't give him that. He gave a slight cough. 'Anyone got any change?'

The man held up a hand. 'Oh, it's all right, we don't take tips. Just wondered if I could stand by that fire a minute and warm up. Maybe have a cup of whatever you're drinking?'

'Oh. Yeah, course.'

The man accepted a drink and then asked for a slice of pizza. Then he helped himself to another, and another. Then he stretched back in the chair, crossed his legs, and shut his eyes.

The friends looked at each other with startled expressions. What's he doing, Spike thought? He can't just stay here. He's the pizza man.

Meatball approached the figure, now starting to doze. 'Er, sorry mate, but haven't you got to be back at work? Or something?'

The man shook his head. 'Nah.'

Spike stared. What? What did this guy think he was doing?

'Well, you can't stay here,' Billy said. 'This is private. Clear off.'

'Billy!'

'Well, none of you lot were saying anything.'

To their surprise, the man suddenly burst into laughter. 'Your faces!'

They stared at him, dumbfounded at the sudden change in his voice.

The man was still laughing. 'If you could've seen your faces when I ate that pizza.'

Spike rose unsteadily from his chair and walked across to face him. It couldn't be. He sounded like Duke, but he couldn't be … could he? '*Duke?*'

'I thought that was your voice,' Meatball yelled. 'My God, Duke, that is some disguise.'

Terri squealed with delight. 'That's not a disguise, is it, Duke? Something that good takes hours. There's something you're not telling us.'

Duke bounded to his feet. 'Look, watch this. I only discovered I could do it this morning.'

He began to change, his features melting slowly back to the Duke they knew.

Billy walked around him, staring in disbelief. '*Wow!* What a skill!'

41

Doc's mouth hung open. '*You can morph.*'

'I don't believe it,' Meatball muttered. 'It's amazing!'

Duke beamed. 'Cool, eh?'

Cool, Spike thought? It's unbelievable.

Doc prodded Duke's arm. 'Cool? It's flaming fantastic! You lucky devil.'

Terri stared at him, shaking her head. 'That must have so freaked you out the first time.'

'Freaked don't come anywhere near it,' Duke said. 'I nearly wet myself. I thought I was going mad.'

He related the story of the beard.

Meatball thumped Duke on the shoulder. 'Now *that*,' he said, 'has got to come in useful.'

Perched on a chair, Spike listened, but kept his thoughts to himself. Meatball was right, that could be very useful, but why now?

CHAPTER SEVEN

'Right,' Duke said, walking across the room. 'Let's look at what we've got so far.'

Almost recovered from Duke's party trick, they sat around the table in Meatball's basement, going over the events of recent days.

'The signs,' said Terri, remembering the exploding sign in the photograph. 'There was the sign for radiation in the photo we took of Brett Tyler. And it was purple, which is a bit too much of a coincidence.'

'The sign. Yeah.' Duke counted it off on his fingers. 'Then …'

'The Christmas card!' Billy yelled. 'The one for me and Spike with the funny verse in it.'

'Yep, the card. That's two.'

'The woman I saw,' said Meatball. 'That was weird. Probably nothing, though.'

'I don't know, Meatball, when you see something, you see it for a reason,' Doc said. 'Remember last time, with that dream? It took a while, but everything you saw happened in the end.'

'Yeah.' Meatball nodded. 'Yeah, it did.'

Spike pondered over the dream Meatball had had the previous year: the dream that had rapidly turned into more of a nightmare. Now he'd seen this vision of a woman walking away: a woman in uniform. What was all that about?

Terri interrupted his thoughts. 'The purple flash in the sky. Don't forget that.'

Duke stroked his chin. 'Which probably means a time portal. So, that's four. And now we suspect Gullivan's back, which is also too much of a coincidence.'

43

'It's him, all right,' Spike said. 'And he'll be the one using the time portal, which means he's up to something.'

'And he was the key to our mission last year,' Doc said, bending down to stroke Gus's huge body. 'It was our destiny to follow him through, so that means our first job is to find this new time portal and keep watch on it, see if it's him using it.'

'Which means we follow him.'

'If we can find him. We didn't have much luck the other day.'

Spike tapped his nose. 'He's back, all right. This never lets me down.'

'*Hello?*'

He turned to look at Terri, who was glancing around the ceiling. 'Hello, what?'

She looked back at him. 'Did you hear something then?'

'No?'

'Hear what, Terri?'

'Oh, nothing, Bill, I just thought I heard … maybe I didn't,' she added, vaguely.

She frowned back up at the ceiling and then shook her head and sat down in her chair, looking slightly mystified.

Doc was watching her. 'You all right, Terri?'

'Mmm? Oh, yes, thanks Doc, yes, I'm ok.'

Spike, too, was watching her. He'd seen her have these odd moments before: moments when she drifted off into her own little world. Surely she wasn't still worrying about the light in the sky?

He turned to face the others. 'Where were we?'

'We were talking about my brilliant idea,' Billy said.

'What brilliant idea?'

'The one I've just had,' said Billy, grinning. '*I* think maybe someone else is using the portal.'

'It's possible, I suppose,' said Meatball. 'We're assuming it's Gullivan using it but, of course, it might not be.'

'He might have a partner,' Duke suggested.

'A partner?' Spike spluttered. 'Him? Who'd want him?'

Meatball chuckled. 'Someone with no sense of smell.'
Duke sighed. 'I meant a business partner. Maybe,
wherever he is, he's met someone who's as evil as he is.' He
clicked his fingers. '*And* knowing the gangsters might still be
after him, he wouldn't want to risk coming back himself.'
Doc paused halfway through spooning chocolate into
some cups and waved the teaspoon in the air. 'That's a good
point.'
Terri sat bolt upright. 'Oh my goodness,' she squealed. 'I
was right!'
'Right about what?'
'*Hello! Yes, I can hear you!* I can't believe it! *I knew it!*'
They swung around. Terri was holding her chin in her
hands.
'Knew what?'
Leaping to her feet, Terri grabbed Spike's arm and started
shaking it. 'I was right! I knew I could hear something!'
'What? What are you talking about, what can you hear?'
Terri stared straight ahead. 'Yes ... yes, I can hear you!'
'Terri? Who are you talking to?'
Seeming not to hear their questions, Terri was almost
laughing with delight.
'Something's wrong with Terri!' Billy yelled.
Meatball got up from his chair. 'Terri, you ok?'
'I knew it!' she cried, looking at them all, 'I knew it!
Didn't I say? It's *them!* It's *her!*'
Spike stared at her, open mouthed. 'Who?'
'Neeza!'
'What are you talking about?'
'Neeza! It's Neeza, I can hear her in my head. She's
talking to me.'
Duke was shaking his head. 'It can't be.'
'Terri, it can't be.' Doc walked over to where Terri stood.
'Terri, listen, it can't be. Neeza ... all of them. They're
millions of light years away ...'

'I'm not stupid! I know when someone's talking to me, for goodness sake. Yes, yes, we're all fine.' She laughed aloud.

'She's asking how you all are.'

Duke leaned on the table with a thud. 'It's not possible, surely.'

'If Terri says she's talking to Neeza, then she is,' Spike said, firmly. 'She was the only one who could communicate with them by thought, remember. But how on earth?'

Doc was gazing at Terri, watching her intently. 'Don't you see? That's the obvious explanation. The Ishmecs must be back.'

Billy punched the air. 'Yes! Perhaps we'll see them again.'

'Well, they did say we were destined to meet again,' said Meatball, 'but somehow I didn't think ...'

'No way. I wonder why?'

'She'll tell us in a minute,' Doc said.

Everyone waited patiently for Terri to finish her one-sided conversation: a conversation that only she could hear.

'They're coming to see us,' she said, suddenly. 'The Ishmecs. They're back, and coming to see us about something very important. Something they need our help with.'

Billy leaped in the air. 'Yes!'

It summed up how everyone felt, as they remembered their friends from the year before.

Neeza, her brother, Jophan, their father Arisius, and the Elder were friends they'd made in their fantastic adventure through a time portal.

They'd followed Gullivan then, too: followed him through the portal to a steamy, tropical world of dinosaurs.

It was there that they'd first encountered the Ishmecs, an amazing alien race of reptilian people, who'd helped them in moments of great danger, and whom they'd been able to help in return.

Now the Ishmecs were back.

Spike and the others exchanged glances. 'So, what do we do now?'

'Any idea when they're coming, Terri?'

'She didn't say exactly,' Terri replied. 'She just said very soon.'

'I wonder if your gran knows,' Meatball said.

Spike nodded. 'Gran'll know, I bet,' he said. 'And Mr Price.'

'But no one's said anything,' said Doc. She gave Spike a glance. 'They haven't, have they?'

'No,' he said, truthfully. 'Gran must know, but she hasn't said anything. I reckon that means we have to sort it ourselves.'

'And now we think Gullivan's back. Oh no, you don't think … you don't think it's something to do with him? I don't see how …'

Terri's voice trailed away.

'Well, I suppose we won't know for sure till we see Jo and Neeza,' said Meatball.

Spike frowned. 'Yeah, but what are we going to do about Gullivan in the meantime?'

He looked up at Duke and Meatball.

Duke shrugged. 'What can we do? I think we'll have to leave it. At least, for the time being. The Ishmecs are more important. And we're not absolutely sure he is back.'

Oh, he's back all right, Spike thought to himself. He made a mental note to keep a close eye on Gullivan's house whenever he could.

Upstairs, a doorbell echoed down the hallway. They froze.

'Surely, not already?'

Meatball listened to the sound of soft footfalls on the floor above, and sprang into action. 'Oh no, Mum's going!'

In two bounds, he was on the staircase, bursting into the hallway just as his mum was opening the door.

'Mum! Wait!'

His mum turned. 'Yes?'

'I'll get the door, Mum, it's probably for me, it's … *oh!*'

His mum regarded him, curiously. 'You all right, dear?'

He nodded. 'Ok, doesn't matter. Hello, Mrs Watts.'

'Mrs Watts and I are going to the Christmas Fair in the village,' his mum continued. 'Dad's out at his model railway club. There's some cake in the tin if you want it.'

'Ok, Mum. Bye.'

As the door shut behind them, Meatball heaved a sigh of relief. Turning, he stepped slowly down the stairs, pausing on the bottom step to catch his breath.

'It's all right,' he said. 'It wasn't …'

He stopped. There before him, hanging in mid-air in the middle of the room, was a small purple rectangle. It spread swiftly outwards and upwards into a luminescent doorway, throbbing with light.

Through it, stepped two figures: two alien creatures, a little older, but happily familiar, dressed, not as they had seen them last in a practical everyday uniform, but in soft robes of purple and blue.

The first was tall and willowy, long and slender face and skin almost iridescent in the purple light. His reddish-brown eyes regarded them with interest. Standing beside him, his sister was smiling, her face smaller and rounder and her eyelids flicking across her soft amber eyes.

Jophan and Neeza were back.

CHAPTER EIGHT

In the middle of the floor in Meatball's basement, the two figures faced them for a moment, and then Jophan took a step forward and bowed.

At his throat, a translator band pulsed with light as he spoke. 'Our warmest greetings,' he said. 'We are delighted to see you all once more.'

Beside him, Neeza pulled a face. '*Jo*,' she said. 'These are our friends.'

'And, as the eldest, I represent Father and Grandfather and the Ishmec people,' he snapped.

Spike rolled his eyes. 'You were right, Terri. It is them.'

Terri giggled.

'It's so good to see you again,' Neeza cried, as she rushed to greet them. 'We have so much to tell you.'

'All right, mate?' Spike stepped towards Jophan and held up his hand. Jophan stared at it for a moment, his eyelids swishing rapidly across his eyes, and then he struck Spike's hand with his own.

'I have remembered,' he announced, greeting Duke, Meatball, and Billy in the same manner.

'Just as well,' said Duke, watching as the girls embraced. 'We don't do hugging.'

Jophan pulled himself up to his full height. 'Nor I,' he said. He gazed intently at Spike's shaved head, previously covered in sharply gelled dark spikes. 'Your hair?'

'Had it cropped. You know, shaved off.'

'Me n'all,' Billy piped up.

Jophan put a hand to his own gleaming head and slid it over his bald leathery skin. 'I also,' he said.

They laughed aloud.

'It's so good to see you all again,' Neeza said. 'We have missed you all ...'

She broke off, looking across at Spike and Billy. 'Terri has told me,' she said, quietly. 'Ed's spirit has passed over.'

Jophan nodded. 'He was excellent. We join with you both in your sadness.'

Spike nodded, uncomfortably. 'Yeah, thanks.'

At that moment, over on the rug by the fireplace, a very warm Gus stretched from tip to tail in one long, sinuous movement. Jophan and Neeza watched in fascination as the huge mound of flowing fur detached itself from the rug, sat up, and gazed at them through large blue eyes.

Jophan drew in a breath. 'Who is this?'

'This is Gus,' said Meatball. 'He's my ...our cat.'

'A cat?'

'He's very friendly,' said Meatball. 'You can stroke him if you like.'

Obviously, the idea had already occurred to Gus, who with another stretch, wandered over to greet them.

Jophan bent down to run a hand through the silky fur. 'He is of such ... he is amazing.' He turned his face to them, full of wonder. 'I, too, would like such a cat.'

Neeza crouched down, her hands cupped around Gus' face. 'This is a creature of great intelligence,' she said, brightly.

The friends knew at once that she must be speaking the truth. They had witnessed her power of understanding with animals many times. It was a skill common to the Ishmec people: a gift that had quickly put Ed at ease at their first meeting.

Jophan stood up. 'Our father sends his greetings and asks if you will grant him audience. We were all to have a little time together first and then he was to follow. He wishes to speak with you on a matter of grave importance.'

'Course.' Duke stepped forward. 'Terri told us you needed our help.'

'You are correct,' he said. 'Though we know few details as yet.'

'We have heard …'

Neeza hesitated, glancing at her brother, then continued softly, 'There is rumour that we are to assist you. Jo and I.'

'It was overheard, nothing more,' said Jophan. 'A mention by Grandfather only. But if it is so …' His eyes lit up. 'But we must wait. Father will explain when he arrives.'

Meatball rushed up the basement steps to the door and drew the bolt across. 'Just in case Mum pops back for anything,' he explained. 'She'll faint if she sees you two, let alone your dad.'

It was not a moment too soon. Over in the corner of the room, another glistening rectangle appeared, stretched into a large doorway, and set in position. Through this, dressed in a flowing robe of purple and silver, stepped the towering figure of their final visitor, Arisius.

They'd forgotten how tall he was; slender and lean and aristocratic, Jophan and Neeza's father had a commanding, yet kindly, presence. His head was large and noble with broad-set eyes and short nose and his leathery skin stretched tightly over prominent cheekbones. He had appeared a little daunting at their first meeting, but now they knew him to be someone of courage, wisdom and compassion: someone they could trust and depend upon.

'My friends!' Arisius stepped forward to greet them. 'It is good to see you all once more. I trust we find you in good health?'

'Thank you, Sir, we are well,' Duke replied.

Arisius spent a few moments greeting each of them in turn. 'And this,' he said, at last. 'This is?'

He turned his attention to Gus, who had been busily sniffing around and now dozed lazily at Neeza's feet.

Meatball stared down at Gus, who had opened his eyes but remained motionless. Almost apologetically, he said, 'He … um … he's a bit independent.'

Spike was a little surprised at Gus' response to Arisius' presence. Ed hadn't done that, he'd taken to Arisius immediately. The year before, at their first meeting, Ed had just trotted off and walked along by his side as though he'd known him for years and trusted him just as long.

Arisius smiled. 'There is no need for apologies,' he said. 'The cat is the king of beasts. I shall go to him.'

'He is of such intelligence, Father,' Neeza cried, as Arisius stepped nearer.

At his approach, Gus stood up. Arisius inclined his head slightly and then put out a hand.

With great care and deliberation, Gus slid his head beneath and let it rest for several moments.

'This is a noble creature indeed,' Arisius said, rising up, 'a soul of great intellect and wisdom.' He looked up at Meatball. 'You are most fortunate. You must take great care of him.'

Meatball watched as Gus settled back down on the rug, gave an enormous yawn, graced them all with a look, and then flopped back to sleep. 'He's also very lazy,' he muttered. 'Guess that enormous brain of his gets tired.'

Smiling, Arisius straightened up.

'Now,' he said, 'let us be seated. We have matters to discuss.'

They sat down around the table.

'How is the Elder, is he well?' asked Terri.

Arisius smiled down at her. 'Thank you for your concern. My father's body is frail, but his mind and soul are strong. He regrets he cannot be with us today, but sends you his greetings.'

Duke began tentatively, 'Jophan and Neeza have told us you require our help, Sir. It is something to assist you and your people?'

'That statement is at once correct, yet incorrect,' Arisius answered. 'Yes, your help is required, but on this occasion, you will be assisting your own people. With some help from us.'

Spike started. 'Our own people? You mean *our* race? *We are in danger?*'

'Yes,' he said. 'An event of disastrous proportions could shortly occur. An event that, if not prevented, has the potential for loss of human life and world-wide contamination.'

A stunned silence fell over the group.

Terri leaned forward. 'We ... *us*?'

'Your people,' Arisius confirmed, gravely. 'An event that will take place but a short distance from where we are now.'

Meatball sat back with a jolt. 'Near *here*?'

Spike felt his mouth gape open.

'Why isn't anyone doing something about it, then?' Billy asked.

'Probably because no one has any idea it's about to happen, Bill, that's why,' Doc said. 'Like lots of other things.'

Spike stood up and walked across the floor, thoughts crowding his mind. A disaster? Loss of human life? Their world, their beautiful world, contaminated? *No...*

For the first time, he realised how the Ishmecs must have felt when there was a possibility they might not be able to leave the earth before the asteroid hit.

He, Billy and their friends had helped them then, undertaking a perilous journey delivering the crystal vital for the drive of their ship, to enable them to leave this planet. They'd done what was asked of them and more, even at the risk of their own lives, but through it all, not really appreciated how the Ishmecs must have felt.

Now, faced with their own possible fate, Spike had some idea.

One ray of hope remained. If it wasn't possible to alter events, why had Arisius sought them out?

'What is the danger?' he asked.

'Less than two miles from here there is a Stately Home,' Arisius began. 'Blackwater Manor.'

'We know that,' Meatball cried. 'Dad works there.'

'Your father? He works in the Stately Home?'

'He's the Estate Manager.'

Arisius nodded. 'I see. He works below ground also?'

Meatball stared at him. 'Below ground?'

'Below ground,' Doc repeated. 'Then ... there's something else there?'

Arisius nodded again. 'There is. Deep underground, beneath Blackwater Manor, there is a secret establishment: a vast network of research facilities where they seek to develop an experimental nuclear reactor. This reactor will shortly malfunction and, due to operator error, will go critical and explode with a potentially devastating effect.'

'But surely there's some way to stop it?'

'There is only one way the catastrophe can be averted,' Arisius said. 'You must place a crystal beneath the reactor chamber.'

Doc leaned forward. 'A crystal? You mean like the crystal we returned to you at the ship?'

'The crystal is of a similar nature but has the capacity to absorb and retain all radiation from the explosion, rendering the area safe and returning it to normal.'

'So, we have to enter the facility and place the crystal in the reactor chamber,' Spike said.

'*No*. The crystal needs merely to be located *beneath* the reactor chamber,' Arisius said. 'At the critical moment, it will envelop the entire reactor chamber, absorbing the radiation and returning it to normal.'

'But surely,' Terri asked, 'won't they know? The scientists and everyone? They'll be aware something is going wrong, and they'll put it right ... won't they?'

'I'm afraid, in this instance, they will not do so. The reactor is still in the experimental stage and there is an aspect that remains inadequately monitored. Due to a computer malfunction, no one will be aware of the danger until it is too late.'

Arisius continued, 'The task that lies before you will be complex and dangerous. Once you have negotiated your way into the establishment itself, you must find your way to the maintenance and access shaft and put the crystal in position. The crystal will turn white when you have positioned it correctly.'

He paused for a moment to look at them. 'Whatever happens,' he said, 'the crystal *must* be in position beneath the reactor chamber by 4.30 p.m. your time, on December 22nd.'

'December 22nd? But that's Friday.'

'That is correct. You must then make your way back down the shaft. When the crystal has completed its work, you will need to retrieve it and return it to us.'

'I guess … I suppose it'll be safe, then, will it? The crystal?'

He nodded. 'The crystal will be completely sealed and may be handled without danger. There is, however, another possibility of which you must be aware. The action of the crystal may have an adverse effect. It may cause distortion in the fabric of time.'

'In what way?'

Arisius looked across at Duke. 'Time itself may be altered by the explosion, and the way you entered the facility may no longer be open to you. At best, you may have to find another way out.'

'And at worst?' asked Meatball, an all too familiar sense of unease creeping up on him.

Arisius looked grave. 'At worst,' he said, 'you may have to find another way back to this place … and this time.'

CHAPTER NINE

Visitors.

In the resonating stillness of his former home in the present day, Cornelius Gullivan stood in the hallway, looking down at several new prints on the dusty floor. Somehow, at some point, someone had been inside the house.

He stared closely at the footprints, and ran through the options in his mind. It could be some kind of vagrant, tramps or a couple of squatters who thought the house was unused. But in this weather they would likely still be in the house and he'd done a thorough search and found no one.

There were other possibilities, of course. Those interfering brats from the old lady's place and their friends, for instance. It wasn't the first time those brats had made a nuisance of themselves, walking all over his land and sticking their noses in to what didn't concern them. Probably with that mutt of theirs too.

But if it was them, why were they here?

Normally, he'd have considered paying them a little visit, especially that spiky-haired kid. He was the ringleader all right.

No. As things were, it was best to keep his head down. It wouldn't do to draw attention to his presence in the house, because the one thing he did not know was the whereabouts of Molly McKendrick and that thug of hers.

Right now, everything was going very nicely indeed and they were the last people he wanted to see. If the McKendricks turned up, it might be the last time he saw anything.

Gullivan gave a long sigh. He needed a drink.

Walking into the kitchen, he grabbed a bottle from the kitchen table and put it to his lips. Empty.

In a fit of rage, he threw the bottle against the wall, showering the sink with fragments and then glanced at the clock. That place in the village was still open, but could he risk it?

'Good evening, sir, just these today for you, is it? Isn't it dreadful weather? I can't remember snow this bad since …'

The voice of the assistant droned on, filtering through the hood pulled forward over Gullivan's face.

'And a hundred blue,' he growled, through the scarf covering his nose and mouth.

'A hundred, sir?' The assistant reached behind him to the display of cigarettes. 'Only got eighty, I'm afraid, sir. I could have a look …'

'That'll do,' Gullivan snapped.

He pulled a wad of cash from his pocket and peeled off several notes, his sharp eyes keeping a careful watch around him as he waited impatiently for his change. Then, snatching up his bag, he left the shop and began the long walk down the road to the lane that led home.

It was becoming cold again. A biting wind bit at his nose and the tips of his ears, even through the thick woollen scarf. How he despised British winters. As soon as he had made enough money, he'd be off abroad to somewhere hot.

Plunging his hands as deeply as he could into his pockets, he stomped along the lane as it skirted the edge of the fields.

At that moment, through the swirling snowflakes, a shape caught his eye. It was a dog: a great muscled thing, all hair, and legs, crashing through the snow in his direction.

That mutt! It was that damned mutt that belonged to those kids. Wait a minute … no, it wasn't. It was similar, but now it grew closer he could see it wasn't him.

'Mason! Mason, come here, boy!'

The voice carried through the icy air, and a figure appeared in the far distance.

Swiftly, Gullivan slipped behind some trees. He didn't know who it was, but he wasn't in the mood to meet anyone right now.

The figure advanced, clipped a lead onto the dog, and dragged him away. 'Will you come on, it's flaming freezing out here.'

On the far side of two large trees, Gullivan held his breath. That voice was familiar.

Bending down, the man ruffled the dog's head and stood up, looking into the wind. A stray gust lifted the hood from his head, flipping it onto his shoulders.

Gullivan's heart skipped a beat.

It was Toby McKendrick.

CHAPTER TEN

'Munitions?'

Doc, Duke and Meatball stood at the oak table in the reference library the next day, looking through a large, heavy book.

'That's what it says here.' Doc pointed to a long piece of text beneath a picture of Blackwater Manor. 'It says during the war Blackwater Manor was used as a munitions factory. Arms and things, you know, where they made weapons. Oh, but wait a minute …'

She lifted the page carefully and turned it over. 'Looks like it was a bit more than that,' she said. 'It looks as though there were underground chambers of some sort, quite deep underground.'

'Well, that fits,' said Duke.

Doc ran a finger down the page. 'And according to this,' she said, 'it was used for research, inventing new weapons and all that sort of thing. The whole thing had concrete walls several feet thick. Make it bombproof, I suppose.'

'I don't see how that helps us,' said Meatball. 'We still can't get in. We can hardly go walking in the front door and ask if they can direct us to the secret research establishment.'

Doc chewed her lip. 'No.'

'I don't see why,' Duke said. 'The Manor is open to the public. We could just go in as visitors.'

'And then what,' said Meatball. 'Look at a load of old stuff and walk out again?'

'You never know. There might be a secret passageway or something. There often is in these old houses.'

Doc's face lit up. 'That's probably how your dad gets in, Meatball. Walks in the front door of the Manor and then down through a secret entrance.'

Meatball considered that for a moment. 'Sounds like a spy film,' he said. 'D'you know, I'm starting to see Dad in a completely new light.'

'The fact remains though,' Doc went on, 'They couldn't have brought weapons out that way during the war, could they?'

Duke frowned. 'No. You'd need something pretty large to bring out weapons.'

'A *tunnel*,' the three of them said together. 'There's got to be a tunnel.'

Duke rubbed his chin. 'Now, where can we find out information about a tunnel?'

'Maybe it was a rail tunnel,' Doc said. 'That would make sense. Steam trains and stuff.'

'We've still got to find out about it. I know, let's ask the librarian.'

The chief librarian was a stout, balding man with strangely shaped glasses sitting half way down his nose. He didn't seem too enthusiastic about answering questions on Blackwater Manor, especially on the last day before Christmas closing.

'I do wish teachers wouldn't set their students these sorts of projects,' he muttered, irritably. 'If it's steam trains you're wanting, you'd be better off asking Mr Judd at the Local History Museum. If he's there, that is. He's very elderly and he only does a few hours these days. Lord knows why, blowed if I'd work if I didn't have to.' He glanced up at the clock. 'But you'll have to move sharp, it closes early today for the Christmas break. And you mind you talk to him with respect.'

They thanked him, and left.

The Local History Museum was only a few minutes walk away on the edge of the village. Henry Judd, the curator, was soft and very elderly, with wisps of grey hair and startling blue eyes. Despite his age, he remembered a great deal about steam trains and the local lines, and he delved into the archives to produce maps and timetables of the routes.

'What we're really interested in, Mr Judd,' Meatball said, as the curator pulled out dozens of old maps, 'are any lines that ran near Blackwater Manor. You know, during the war.' Mr Judd looked up. 'Oh, you want the wartime lines. Blackwater Manor? That'd be the old Coopers Halt and Goswell Line. That's been out of use for donkey's years. I can show you a map.'

Staring at a shelf for a few moments, he selected a roll of thick paper and unfurled it on the desk, weighting down the corners with various objects.

'Now ... here ... see?' He ran a finger down the line. 'That's the old Coopers Halt line. You can see where it comes off Sedgewick Junction. That was then, of course, you won't find it there now.'

'You mean, there's none of the line left?'

'Well, most of it was closed by Dr Beeching, along with a lot of others in the 60s, but there's still bits about. All overgrown now, of course. There were a few sidings ...'

He went back to the map. 'That one there, look, that runs near the manor, up to there, see? Then it goes underground.'

'Underground?'

'Yes, it goes quite some way underground. Used for munitions during the war. All gone now, of course. All the rails were taken up.'

'What about the tunnel? Is that still there?'

Mr Judd shook his head, vaguely. 'It'll still be there I expect, but probably bricked up. But if you can find it, that's where it'll be.'

He circled an area on the map with his finger. 'Want me to photocopy this for you, kids?'

'That's very kind of you,' Doc said. 'We can print some more and use them for our projects. Thank you, Mr Judd.'

Forty minutes later, with the map tightly rolled in brown paper securely tucked under Meatball's arm, they arrived back at Yew Tree Cottage to find Spike, Terri, and Billy in jubilant mood.

'You mean, you could just see it?' gasped Duke, as they told them. 'Everything he'd seen?'

Terri nodded, looking a little stunned herself by what had happened.

She, Spike and Billy had been talking about getting into the research facility, and through the security system that must obviously be in place when, out of the blue, an idea had popped into Terri's head.

She wasn't sure why she had thought of it, she said, or where the idea had come from, and it sounded ridiculous, but she couldn't resist the urge to give it a try.

Calmly, she'd said, 'Why don't I see if I can contact Gus?'

'Contact Gus?' Spike asked, incredulously. 'He's at work with Meatball's dad. What are you going to do, ring his mobile?'

'I mean, by thought,' she said, quietly. 'I may be able to. It's worth a try, anyway.'

Spike opened his mouth to say, 'How d'you think you're going to do that?' but stopped short. He'd seen more than enough strange things in the last year to convince him that anything was possible, and Terri did have this weird empathy thing with animals going on.

Instead he said, 'Why? What's the point?'

'Well, if I can contact him, he may be able to tell me how we can get in.'

He pulled a face. 'What?'

'I think it's a great idea,' Billy said, still staring at Terri's face. 'I bet she can do it, Spike, I bet she can.'

Spike shrugged. 'Ok,' he said. 'Give it a go if you want.'

So she did. Sitting on the edge of her seat, Terri closed her eyes and thought about Gus, while Billy and Spike sat and watched. Several moments passed and nothing happened.

Then, suddenly she spoke. 'I've got him,' she whispered. 'I've got him.'

Billy grabbed her hand. 'You're talking to him? You're talking to Gus like you did with Jo and Neeza?'

'It's better than that,' she said, happily. 'I can see everything he's seen.'

She tapped her forehead. 'It's here,' she said. 'In my head. I can see where Gus went this morning and what he's seen.'

Turning her head to look up at Spike, she said, 'I can see how we get in, Spike. Through the security and everything. I can see Meatball's dad tapping in codes on the doors.'

Despite everything, Spike almost fell into a chair. 'I don't believe it. That is absolutely *brilliant*.'

Duke's mouth dropped open as Terri finished telling them her story.

'Incredible,' Doc said, shaking her head in disbelief. 'Talk about useful.'

Meatball grasped Terri's arm. 'Dad was tapping in *codes*? Then he does work underground? *Wow* ...'

'Looks like it,' she said.

'That's fantastic,' said Duke. 'Now all we have to do is get in. We had a bit of luck at the museum.'

Meatball unrolled the map of the railway line and spread it out for them to see. 'Now, Mr Judd said this is the line that ran to the Manor, and it goes underground somewhere here.'

He circled a small area.

'I suppose it is still there, is it? The tunnel?'

'Well, Mr Judd seems to think it probably is, but it might be bricked up or something.'

'What do we do if it is?'

'Don't know, Bill,' Spike said. 'But somehow we have to find a way in. We have to get inside with that crystal or we're done for.'

'What if it doesn't work?' Terri asked. 'What do we do, then?'

A cold chill washed over Spike as he considered the question, and realised just how precious ordinary, everyday life could be.

'It has to,' Duke muttered in desperation, 'it has to work. We have to get the crystal inside that place and it has to work. If not, well ...'

They turned to look as a purple light blossomed in the space, which expanded and stretched into a large doorway, and the smiling figures of Jophan and Neeza stepped through and back into the room.

'We are to accompany you,' Jophan said, excitedly. 'It is permitted.'

'Yes!'

'That's brilliant,' Duke said, as they crowded around.

'That is the best news ever,' said Spike. He stopped to stare at them. 'Whoa!' he cried. 'You got jeans!'

Jo and Neeza beamed, pulling at their new clothes.

'These are made to look like your clothes,' said Neeza proudly. 'It was deemed wise.' She held out her arm. 'And we have coats too. You see?'

Doc laughed as she looked them up and down. 'You look completely different. Oh wow!'

'You look amazing,' said Meatball. 'How d'you like wearing our stuff?'

'It does not feel the same as your fabric,' Jophan said. 'Your fabric would irritate our skin. It merely appears the same.'

Terri leaned across to feel Neeza's jumper. It felt soft and warm. 'That's so clever,' she said.

Jo held out his coat for them to touch. The fabric was soft and doughy, almost mouldable. Their fingers left trails in the surface, which immediately smoothed over.

'That's incredible,' Duke said. 'Like all your stuff. You'd never know the difference.'

'The fabric is also very warm,' Jophan continued. 'It will retain our body heat. The temperature here ...'

He looked out at the snow.

'Yeah, it's really cold here,' said Spike. 'You get used to it.'

'Doesn't mean we like it, though,' Terri said. 'I can't wait for the summer.'

'And me,' said Doc. She closed her eyes for a moment. 'Can't wait to be sitting on a beach, eating ice cream.'

Jo and Neeza looked at them.

'You've got to try it,' said Billy.

'We haven't got any now,' Meatball said. He grinned. 'But we have got some doughnuts ...'

'S'pose that'll have to do,' said Spike.

'Oh, Spike doesn't want one.' Meatball laughed. 'All the more for us.'

He reached into the cupboard and pulled out several bags. 'Now this one is your plain jam doughnut,' he said, showing it to Jo and Neeza. 'And these are caramel, chocolate and custard.'

'Caramel's mine,' said Duke.

'Guests first, greedy-guts,' Terri said, sharply.

Duke watched as the doughnuts were passed around, keeping a careful watch on the caramel.

They settled down on the chairs for a while, chatting and talking about mundane, everyday things, everything except the mission that lay ahead. Spike was glad to forget about it for a moment: glad to forget the worrying thought going around in his mind.

Somehow, they had to get this right. They had to.

CHAPTER ELEVEN

'Hang on,' said Meatball. 'Where's the crystal?'

Spike stared at Jophan. 'Yeah, where is the crystal? Weren't you supposed to bring it with you?'

Jophan and Neeza grinned at each other.

'We have brought the crystal,' he said.

'Where is it, then?'

'There!' yelled Billy. 'I bet that's it!' He pointed at Neeza. Around her throat, on a golden chain, hung a small pyramid of purple crystal.

'That?' Terri gasped. 'That's it?'

'*That's* the crystal?'

'I thought it would be like the other one,' Duke said. 'I thought we'd have to carry it.'

Doc moved across to have a closer look. '*Incredible*,' she breathed. 'This little thing will absorb all that radiation?'

Neeza nodded. 'Grandfather has said it is so. This crystal has great power. It will do everything that is required.'

Duke peered at the crystal in astonishment. 'It's so tiny.'

'Father says the smallest things are often the most powerful,' said Jophan.

'Amazing,' said Meatball. 'We won't even have to carry it.'

'And it'll fit into a tiny space,' said Doc. 'Which might be really useful when we get there.'

Billy stood up and started walking around, impatiently. 'When are we going, then?'

'Soon, Bill, we have to make sure we've got everything. We'll need a torch.'

'Gran's got a couple of new ones out in the shed,' Spike said. 'I'm sure she won't mind us borrowing them.'

'There's this one,' Meatball said, dipping into the pocket of his jacket, 'but it might be dead. I used it the other night.' He slid the button. A weak beam of yellowing light splayed across the ceiling. 'I'll put a new battery in it.'

'The crystal will provide illumination,' Jophan said, eagerly.

'Will it?'

'Most certainly.'

'We may not be able to use that everywhere, though,' said Terri. 'It'll be seen.'

'And it'll make people look at Neeza,' Billy said. 'And we don't want that.'

There was silence.

'What?' Billy shrugged. 'Well, we don't, do we?' He paused, awkwardly. 'Well, they don't look like us, do they? People are going to notice. Sorry.'

He glanced across at Jo and Neeza, but Jophan was slowly nodding.

'It is of no consequence,' he said. 'You are completely correct, Billy. We shall indeed be noticed.'

'Yeah, it's a good point,' said Meatball. 'It's no problem though, is it? Look, it's freezing cold out. They can borrow a couple of hoodies from us and a couple of scarves across their faces. It'll only leave their eyes.'

Spike glanced at Jophan's bright orange eyes, just as the reptilian eyelids slid smoothly across like a crocodile's. Billy was right, he thought, they were going to be noticed. The hoodies and scarves would help, but their eyes were weird.

'We'll just have to hope for the best,' he said.

'It's a bit gloomy out today, anyway,' Doc chipped in. 'If they keep their heads down no one will see them.'

'Right,' said Duke. 'Is that everything? Grab two torches, a couple of scarves and two hoodies.'

By the time they left Yew Tree Cottage, the gloom of winter was beginning to creep in. The heavy, silver-grey clouds that had broken briefly that morning allowing a flash of sunlight to sparkle on the snow, were now closing in again, enveloping the countryside in a suffocating stillness.

A slight wind teased its way into Spike's hood to nip his ears as they set off down the road into the village. It was well trodden, crisp, and slippery and the few puddles had already solidly refrozen.

'It's going to snow again, isn't it?' Doc said. 'Just our luck.'

'Might be good,' said Meatball, righting himself after a slide on a long stretch of glossy snow. 'Might give us a bit of cover.'

'That's true,' Duke said. 'With that and the Christmas Fair, we should be ok. There'll be loads of people about.'

'Oh.'

'What?'

'I've just thought,' said Meatball. 'Mum might be there as well. We'd better make sure we don't bump into her. You know what she's like, she's bound to want to meet our friends.'

Spike tugged on the strings of his hood. 'Then we make sure we keep away from the Fair,' he said. 'Let's go round the outside of the village, up past the green. Then we can take the old road up onto Temperance Hill. Where did Mr Judd say the tunnel might be?'

'Let's have a look at the map, Duke.'

Duke pulled the roll of paper from his inside pocket and zipped his coat again quickly.

'Right.' Terri jabbed her finger on the paper. 'There's the church, and that's over on the hill there. So looking at it from here ...'

'If this is where the tunnel starts, we've got a bit of a walk,' Doc interrupted. 'Look, it starts right over there.'

'Father says Blackwater Manor is two miles in distance,' Jophan said.

'So, judging by the map, the tunnel must be about a mile long,' said Terri, nervously. 'Great. I don't fancy that. It's going to be dark and full of horrible stuff.'

'There's bound to be spiders 'n' everything,' said Billy.

'And rats,' Doc said. 'Might even be snakes.'

Terri shivered. 'Oh, shut up!'

Neeza stretched out a gloved hand to touch Terri's arm. 'There will be no darkness,' she said. 'We have the crystal. The crystal will light our way.'

'Really?'

Neeza nodded as best she could behind a face half covered in a scarf and a very tight hood. 'I am sure.'

'Ok, let's get going,' said Spike. 'It's bound to start snowing again soon. Be better if we can get to the tunnel before it gets worse.'

Duke pushed the map back inside his coat. 'We'll keep to this road. Jo, Neeza, you ok?'

'We are ok,' Jophan replied.

They walked on along the icy road skirting the very edge of the village. The distant sounds of Christmas carols and voices faded in and out, as they walked down past the green, beside the frozen village pond and the rowan trees bowed down with snow.

Faint traces of snowflakes were dancing on the air as they rounded the corner past the brook and the little wooden bridge towards the deserted railway station, long since disused now the track had been diverted through Sedgewick Junction, and a brand-new station built nearby.

By the time they neared the old station car park, the flakes were thicker, and their ears and noses were beginning to sting. The long walk up Temperance Hill lay ahead.

'Oh look … it's snotty Collins and his little friends.'

Spike's heart sank. He knew that voice. Brett Tyler. Just what they didn't need.

'Ignore him,' said Meatball. 'Keep walking.'

'What's up, Collins? Ain't you talking?' Brett tried to push against him.

'Keep going,' Duke urged.

Deep in his pocket, Spike could feel his fist clenching, but he kept on walking.

'Ere, Brett …'

One of Brett's thugs jogged alongside them. 'They've got some new friends with them, look.'

'Eh?' Brett peered around the edge of the group. 'Oh, *yeah*. So they have. Who are you, then?'

Closing in protectively around Jophan and Neeza, the friends hurried on, trying desperately to ignore the taunts of Brett and his gang, but still they kept coming.

'Oi! I'm talking to you!' Brett roared the words through the tumbling snowflakes and then, getting no response, he lunged forward and grabbed Jophan's shoulder, pulling him around.

The others rushed to help him, but Jophan stood his ground. Turning to face Brett, he slowly pulled down his scarf, raised his head, and stared long and hard into Brett Tyler's face.

In the dark hollow beneath Jophan's hood was the bald, skeletal head, the shimmer of reptilian skin, the glowing, almost luminous, orange eyes, and the *swish-swish* of crocodilian eyelids.

Spike watched Brett's mouth fall open, as his face drained of colour, and he dropped the snowball he held in his free hand and froze where he stood.

'What is it, Brett, what's going on?'

The rest of his gang gathered round as Brett stood, looking shell-shocked. One of his gang reached out and grabbed him.

'What's up?'

They turned to stare at Jophan's retreating back, as together with Spike and the others, he ran off as fast as he could.

Another gang member shook him. 'They're getting away. Brett, they're getting away …'

'He's …'

Another member of the gang shook him hard. 'What the hell are you doin'?

'*Him*!' Brett suddenly snarled, jabbing a finger in Jophan's direction. 'That friend of theirs is some kind of weirdo!'

'What d'you mean?'

'He's *scared* ...'

'No, I ain't!' Brett yelled. 'He's wearing some kind of mask! Nobody looks like that! Get him!'

The five members of Brett's gang bounded off in pursuit. Brett Tyler hesitated, then pulled himself together and followed.

'You don't scare me, you freak!' Brett screamed. 'Nobody looks at me like that! I'll have you!

CHAPTER TWELVE

Slightly ahead, Duke and Meatball raced across the car park, trying to keep their grip on the slippery surface, with Terri, Doc, and Neeza following close behind and Billy stumbling along between Spike and Jophan.

Terri glanced over her shoulder. 'They're catching up!'

'We've got to keep going!' Duke yelled.

'In the station!' Spike cried. 'Get in the old station!'

'*Wait*!'

Neeza had stopped and was now pulling on the chain around her neck. 'I must stop!'

'We have to keep going,' yelled Duke, 'they're getting nearer.'

'I must stop,' she pleaded.

Jophan rushed to her side. 'There is a problem?'

'The crystal, Jo,' she panted. 'It is … it is telling me something.'

Carefully, she eased the crystal from inside her coat and looked at it. It was glowing with a curious light.

'What's it doing?' asked Terri.

'You never know with those crystals,' said Meatball.

Jophan clutched Neeza's arm. 'You must do what it instructs.'

Neeza nodded, then moving to stand behind the group, she closed her eyes and held the crystal high in the air.

Looking down the lane, Spike watched Brett and his gang getting nearer. 'Whatever it's going to do, it had better be quick.'

At that moment, a beam of purple light burst from the crystal, soared through the icy air until it reached Brett Tyler and his gang, and then, in one flowing movement, it fanned out and spread across their path like a translucent curtain. It was too late to stop and wonder: too late to avoid it. Brett Tyler and his gang ran headlong into the purple curtain and found themselves captured like flies on a paper. Shock and surprise on their faces, they flailed about, desperately trying to free themselves, but their arms and legs held fast, dragging aimlessly through the air in slow motion.

Stunned, the others watched in disbelief.

'It's grabbed them!' Billy's mouth gaped open. 'Look at that! They can't *move*.'

Duke stared at it. 'Oh wow …'

'Oh my God.' Doc sighed. 'That crystal is phenomenal.'

Terri turned to Neeza who was smiling, a hand to her mouth. 'That is so clever,' she said. 'How did you do it?'

'I do not know,' she replied. 'I simply knew what must be done. But we must hurry, it may not be effective for long.'

Leaving Brett and his gang still trapped and squirming helplessly in the curtain, they set off again, slipping and sliding across the car park, and then dashed around the corner and into the old station, sweating, despite the bitter cold.

On up the platform and into the station, past the old ticket box and the empty snack machines, they poured into an archway and stopped to catch their breath.

'We can't … stop here … too long,' gasped Meatball. 'There's no knowing how long that curtain thing will hold them up.'

Spike gripped his side to ease a stitch. 'I'm wondering if it might be a good idea to split up,' he said. 'One lot can draw them off and the others carry on. Might give us a better chance. We can text and meet up as soon as we can.'

Duke nodded. 'Yeah, might be a good idea,' he said. 'Meatball, you, Terri, Billy and me will run on. If we can get a bit of distance …'

He paused to take a long breath, releasing it in clouds of mist. 'We'll go back towards the village and hopefully they'll see and follow us.'

He turned to Spike. 'You lot carry on, but you'll have to hide somewhere till Brett and that lot have gone past. I'll text you as soon as we've shaken them off.'

Painfully, Spike straightened up. 'Right. We'll see you later.'

He watched as, with Meatball leading, Duke, Terri and Billy ran back out onto the platform. Then he and the others darted into the old Waiting Room, slipped into the toilets at the end and dragged a small table against the door. Crouched inside the little room, they watched through the mottled glass of the window, and waited.

It wasn't long before they heard raised voices and the sound of boots running along the platform. Finally free from the curtain and boiling with rage, Brett Tyler and his gang were on the move to hunt them down. Spike dipped quickly below the window ledge as several figures ran past and on up the platform.

He heard Brett's voice, loud and angry. 'Where are they?!'

'Brett! There, look! Over there!'

Raising his head just above the window ledge, he watched Brett swing around to peer at the figures in the distance, who were just disappearing out of sight. 'He's right!' Brett yelled. 'Get 'em!'

Back inside the waiting room, Spike held his breath, watching. The sound of footsteps grew fainter and then faded away as Brett and his gang leapt off the edge of the platform into the snow and set off after Duke and the others.

Slowly, he lifted his head above the windowsill and looked out. 'Looks like they've gone.'

He moved across to the window and looked outside, up and down the platform. Then he walked across, opened the door and leaned out, keeping close to the wall. Brett Tyler and his gang were just visible running up the road.

Jophan appeared behind him. 'The plan has worked,' he said. 'But we must hurry.'

Spike nodded.

'Quick, look at this!' Doc's voice called out to them from inside the waiting room. She was standing by an old railway poster on the far wall.

'We haven't got time to look at pictures,' Spike called, irritably. 'Come on.'

'But ... but Spike, it's moving.'

Pushing through the doorway, he ran over to look. 'What? What you talking about ...'

Jophan and Neeza crowded around to see.

The poster was in a large frame screwed to the wall. The edges were curled and slightly faded, but in the centre, the image was boldly coloured, crisp, and clear. In the picture, in the middle of a scene of rolling countryside, an old steam train was puffing slowly into a tunnel.

Spike's voice dropped to a croak. '*Holy* ...'

Doc stared at him. 'See? It is moving, isn't it? I'm not seeing things, am I?'

Jophan put out his hand and rested it on the glass. 'There is an energy field here,' he said. 'I can feel it.'

He lifted his hand and the steam train chugged slowly out of the other end of the tunnel, black smoke belching from its stack. As the last carriage left the darkness, a radiation sign appeared on the keystone of the tunnel wall, pulsed with purple colour, and exploded.

'A sign,' said Jophan. 'It must be a sign. Perhaps the tunnel we have identified on the map is correct.'

'Then we'd better find it,' Spike said. 'Come on, we'll go out the other door in case they come back.'

They ran across to the door on the opposite side of the waiting room, pulled it open ... and stepped straight into the unknown.

CHAPTER THIRTEEN

The smell was overpowering. It filled Spike's senses, pungent, and cloying. It was the sickly scented aroma of cut timber, and the dank, raw mould of earth.

The four of them were in a warm, round space, standing all at once not on cold, flat, rigid concrete, but on an uneven, trodden floor of compacted soil, surrounded by walls of roughly-hewn wood.

Vast shadows on the walls trembled and shook by the flickering glow of candlelight, the smell of wax mingling with the distinctive smell of paraffin from three small lamps. Traces of cigarette smoke hung in the air.

A battered table in the corner was laden with boxes. Bags lay strewn about the floor.

In the half-light, they stood reeling and gasping in the suffocating odour, clinging to each other for support.

Then, somewhere in the shadows to their left, they heard the loud snap of a shotgun.

'Hello kiddies,' said a rasping voice. 'How nice of you to drop in.'

A cold chill set them shivering. Slowly, they turned around. Sitting before them, on a wooden chair, was a thin, bony figure, filthy and dishevelled, pinched eyes glaring at them down a long nose. The figure leered at them, showing brown stumps of tooth. At his lip, a cigarette glowed with fire.

'Little bit … *lost* are we, then?' Cornelius Gullivan spat out the words.

Disbelieving, Spike stood looking at him, his stomach heavy with dread. Of all the times.

His eyes narrowed. He was right then, Gullivan *was* back. Deep inside, he'd known it, even though he didn't think the others were so sure, but even he hadn't expected to bump into him so soon. Where on earth were they, anyway? Grabbing a lamp, Gullivan stood up and glared at them all. 'Oh, now, that's real cute, ain't it? You brought a couple of them aliens with you.' He ran a dirty hand over his grizzled chin. 'Seem to remember getting rid of a couple of them a while ago.'

Spike felt anger and hatred well up inside him. He remembered exactly how Gullivan had 'got rid' of a couple of the Ishmec race the year before when he'd attacked the Elder and his guards.

Beside him, he felt Jophan start forward. Quickly, he grabbed his arm to restrain him.

'*No.*'

'Damn weirdos,' Gullivan snapped. He leaned forward to stare into Jophan's face. 'And they don't come much weirder than you lot, do they, boy?'

Jophan looked as if Gullivan's foul breath was almost choking him, but feeling Spike's pressure on his arm, he remained still.

'That's right, boy, you'd better listen to your friend here, or I might decide not to be quite so nice. Got it?'

Walking across to one of the boxes, he lifted out a bottle and pulled the cork. Then he took a long swig of the amber coloured liquid and wiped his chin.

'So, where's all your buddies, then? Gone to see Santa? Oi! I'm talking to you!'

'They're on a school trip,' Doc blurted.

Gullivan grunted, then gulped another long draft from the bottle, and sat down on a box. 'Huh,' he said. 'Been nosing around the old railway station, have you? What you doing there?'

'A school project,' Spike muttered. 'We're doing it for homework.'

77

'Oh yeah … bet you wish you'd stayed at home now, don't you?'

He jerked the bottle in the direction of Jophan and Neeza. 'And what about these two freaks? Don't tell me you bumped into them at the shops.'

'We are lost, also,' Jophan said. 'Our ship was off course.'

'Off course?' Gullivan scoffed. 'Yeah, about a million light years off course.' He pushed the shotgun in their direction. '*Now*,' he growled. 'What are you doing here?'

'We are to assist in preventing a nuclear catastrophe,' Neeza said, boldly.

There was a stony silence, then, throwing back his head, Gullivan let out a long hoarse laugh. 'Course you are, sweetie,' he snarled. The smile faded from his face. 'Get over there while I think.'

They moved to stand at the side as Gullivan rose to his feet and began to pace up and down.

Somewhere outside, Spike heard voices.

'Oh, of *course*! You haven't met my new friends, have you?'

He cast Jophan and Neeza a withering glance. 'Can't wait to see what they make of you two. Over there by the door.'

He jerked the shotgun around in the direction of a door cut in the wall. Reaching across, he drew back two bolts and flung it open. 'You can meet my other *guests*,' he growled, thrusting them through the doorway. 'I'm sure they're going to love you lot.'

Spike, Jophan, Doc and Neeza stumbled in a heap through the doorway onto the dank earth of a well-trodden pathway leading away into the darkness. The air echoed with the sounds of the night. Overhead, a brilliant silver moon shimmered in a sky peppered with stars.

'Down the path,' Gullivan snapped, closing the door behind him. 'Go on. I've got a nice little place to put you while I have a think. You might just come in useful.'

Hearts pounding, they walked together down the path, gripping each other tightly for support, conscious of the twin barrels of the shotgun pushing them onwards.

For several terrifying moments, they walked on into the darkness until, just ahead, Spike saw a faint glow.

'Get a move on!'

Gullivan growled at them, pushing them closer to the light. Ahead, a row of timber stakes rose up out of the darkness. To one side, a small fire burned brightly. As they drew nearer, two figures stepped forward out of the gloom and stood before Gullivan, waiting expectantly.

He waved an arm through the air. At once, the figures walked across to a large wooden gate and heaved it open. Inside, the flickering flames of another larger fire spat and crackled. Clouds of dense smoke billowed into the night sky.

'Get in there,' snarled Gullivan. He shoved Spike sharply in the back with the shotgun, and he tumbled forward onto the ground.

Resting the shotgun on his shoulder, Gullivan leaned close into their faces, and snarled, 'Now just keep it shut you little toe rags, or I'll hand you over to him.'

He nodded towards the broad, muscular figure, now hovering by the door. 'Got it?'

Aching with fear and resentment, Spike pushed himself to his feet beside the others, staring at Gullivan's leering face as the door slowly closed.

The smoke from the fire was thick and choking, searing their throats. Shocked, dazed and terrified, their eyes streamed with water. Carefully, they picked their way over the floor and across to the wall, trying desperately to find some fresh air: some relief from the foul stench.

Neeza peered into the gloom at the other inhabitants of the stockade and then crouched down onto her knees. 'Down. We must do as the others do and keep low to the floor. There is little draught in this place. The smoke will rise. We must keep low.'

They copied her, crawling on all fours across the floor and crowding together in a dark corner.

In the smoky gloom, Doc wiped her eyes on her sleeve, and struggled to make some sense of what had happened. 'I don't understand it,' she croaked. 'I mean, how? How did we end up with Gullivan? And where on earth are we?'

'I don't know,' rasped Spike, his throat hot and dry from the smoke. 'I wish I did.'

'I have been thinking,' said Jophan. 'And a connection with the energy field in the poster is the only logical explanation. We could, I venture to suggest, have crossed into another time.'

'The station *door* …'

'The station door. Of course.' Doc stared ahead. 'Jo's right. The station door must be a time portal.'

'Yes.' Jophan nodded. 'Somehow, it is activated by the poster on the wall. There is a definite energy field there.'

Spike nodded slowly. 'That makes sense all right. A time portal through to … wherever *this* is.'

'A time portal that Gullivan has discovered also,' Neeza whispered.

Spike paused for a moment. 'Of course! This must be where he ended up.' He turned to Doc. 'Last time. You remember. Mr Price said Gullivan had gone somewhere else. This must be it. This must be where he's *been* all this time.'

Doc gasped. 'For the last *year*!'

'Yeah.' Spike's eyes narrowed. 'And he's using it to come back home. I knew he'd been back. I knew it was him I could smell!'

'It would appear you were correct,' said Neeza. 'Which means somehow he has discovered about the poster also. But why would he return again? To this unpleasant place? Why keep returning, when he can escape?'

'Because he's up to something as usual,' he said. 'There must be something here he's after. Something valuable …'

'Never mind *that*,' Doc interrupted. 'We now know the door's a time portal, and he's using it. Which means there *is* a way back. There's a way home, and it comes out in the station waiting room.'

'That's right!' he said. 'If we could only get out of this place.'

Jophan nodded. 'There has to be a way. We must concentrate.'

From their place in the dark corner, Spike glanced around the stockade. The fire had mellowed to a crackling glow. The clouds of smoke had quietened into curling wisps drifting on the air.

For the first time, they noted the other occupants: other prisoners. Some were huddled in groups, others alone and dejected. Directly opposite, two men struggled to find any comfort on the hard, straw-covered floor.

Discreetly, Spike stared at them, trying to decide exactly who or what they were. Some kind of soldiers? It was difficult to see in the semi-gloom. Their skin seemed to be dark, and their hair looked black, but of course, everyone looked that way in poor light. All the same, they didn't look British. His glance took in their uniform and footwear. It seemed familiar somehow.

His mind plucked the answer from his memories of history lessons at school. *Romans?* He glanced at their feet. Those sandals were Roman, and Roman uniforms, just like he'd seen in the books. These must be Roman soldiers. What were they called?

As if she'd heard his thoughts, Doc interrupted with the answer. 'They're Romans, Spike. Roman Legionaries.'

'Doc is correct,' Jophan whispered. 'We have seen images of people such as these.'

'Whoever they are, they don't look too good,' Doc hissed. Spike nodded. Even in the flickering light of the fire, it was obvious that the soldiers were close to collapse with fatigue and neglect.

'They have been without nourishment for too long,' Neeza said.

Spike nodded again. Those soldiers been left there without food and little water. Left to die. Gullivan didn't care, why would he? He cared about no one and nothing but himself. The thought worried him. What if he left *them* there, too?

He lifted his eyes to the deep velvet of the sky and gazed on the crystalline stars. They looked like spilt salt on a dark carpet. Billions of stars. He'd never realised before that there were so many.

Lowering his gaze, two rounded objects came suddenly into view, perched high on the tips of two narrow stakes.

Ugh … dear God …

The sickening reality of what he was seeing turned his stomach, and he looked quickly away.

'This is a fearful place,' Jophan said, following his gaze. 'A place of despair. We must plan our escape.'

'There's got to be a way out of this,' Doc said. 'There has to be a way. All we need to do is think. Gullivan can't keep us here for ever. He's got to let us out.'

'Look!'

Neeza grabbed Doc's arm.

Doc looked over at the corner behind them where another soldier lay, half hidden in the straw. *'Oh my goodness …'*

Neeza walked across and stared down at the soldier. 'The unfortunate creature.'

The others joined her.

'He suffers much,' Jophan observed, looking down at the agonised features.

Doc bent closer. In the flickering glow of the firelight, she could just make out the soldier's hand clamped agonisingly over a long, deep gash in his side. Blood oozed thickly around the whole area.

'He has a bad injury,' she said. 'Looks like he's been stabbed or something. Probably one of those swords they've got.'

'Bet it was Gullivan,' Spike muttered.

Neeza looked at the soldier. 'Will he survive?'

At that moment, the soldier gave a faint groan and his face convulsed with pain.

'Not for long, if he doesn't get some help.'

'What can we do?' asked Jophan. He turned to Neeza. 'The crystal? It cannot help?'

Neeza shook her head. 'There is no response from the crystal.'

Doc knelt down by the soldier's side, spread her hands above the surface of the wound, and closed her eyes.

'I can see a white light,' she whispered. 'A brilliant white light. It's filling my head.'

Slowly, she put her hands to her face. 'It's in my hands! It's just poured from my head into my hands! I'm holding it! Like a ball!'

She stared at her hands in wonder and then lowered them slowly until they were just above the wound.

Crouching beside her, Neeza watched, transfixed. 'What is it that you are doing now, Doc?'

'I don't … I don't know,' Doc croaked. 'I just know this is what I have to do.' She took a deep breath. 'The light,' she whispered. 'It's pulsing in my hands. I can see it!'

Watching, Spike's mouth dropped open. 'Where? I can't see anything.'

'I see nothing, either,' Jophan said, softly.

'Doc can,' Neeza gasped, looking into Doc's face. 'She has the gift!'

They continued to watch as Doc slowly opened her hands. 'It's moving,' she said. 'It's pouring onto the wound like liquid …'

A moment passed, and then the soldier's face started to relax.

'It eases him, I think,' Neeza whispered. 'Look at his face.'

'He's healing,' Doc said. 'The wound's mending inside, I can see it! The torn edges are knitting together, and it's all clean! They're not red and swollen anymore.'

She looked up at them, tears in her eyes.

'Look!' Neeza pointed to the slashed flesh exposed through the gaping hole in the soldier's blood-soaked garments.

Dumbfounded, they watched the ragged edges of the wound meld together until it was whole once more. Trembling and exhausted, Doc sat back on her heels and put her shaking hands to her face.

'You've done it!' Spike hissed. 'You've healed him, Doc!

Doc looked down at the soldier, at his face once contorted with pain but now liberated to peaceful serenity and watched tears of relief and gratitude run silently down his cheeks.

His cracked lips slowly parted. From a hoarse throat came one whispered word.

'*Angelus…*'

CHAPTER FOURTEEN

Back in the twenty-first century, Meatball, Duke, Terri and Billy stumbled on to the very end of the station, battling through the heavy snow and then veering off to take the road back to the village.

Duke glanced behind them. Somewhere in the far distance, several dark shapes were faintly visible through the snowflakes. Brett Tyler and his mates were still there. Somehow, they had to get away.

'This way! We can take the shortcut down Bonnetts Lane!'

Ploughing on, Duke's feet felt like lead and his legs were beyond aching. He knew the others must feel the same. Stumbling forward, they reached the end of the narrow lane, before trampling in a rush out into the High Street at the end, and into a square. It was an open place with trees and a frozen fountain, with few people and even fewer places to hide.

Slowing to a jog, Meatball looked up at the street lamps faintly glowing with the first pink tinges of light.

'We have to find somewhere to hide,' he puffed, 'until we're sure we've shaken them off.'

'The cinema!' Billy cried.

'If we've got any money,' Duke said.

'We can get in through the old side door,' said Billy. 'No one'll see us in this weather.'

Meatball bent over to rest on his knees, struggling to catch his breath. 'We'll have to, Duke. I think it was them I saw turning into the bottom of the lane behind us. They're bound to catch up.'

Stomping down the High Street, they made for the Embassy cinema which, by some miracle, was still open. It was a very old cinema run by a group of enthusiasts. The screen was smaller than the newer, larger cinema complex in the town and poorly lit, and it was a simple matter to slip softly in through the old side door.

They managed to creep quietly up the stairs and sit down in a row between several groups of people, and then tugged on their hoods and held their breath.

In silence, they sat like statues in the din of the movie soundtrack.

All was quiet, save for the voices and action on screen and the occasional laughter from the audience, and then, out of the blue, the side door swung open with a deafening crash onto the wall inside, causing gasps and cries of astonishment.

'Ssh!'

Creeping slowly up the staircase, Brett Tyler peered along the rows. In the opposite gangway, another of his friends scanned the seats, staring intently.

A burst of laughter sprang around the audience. In the middle, Duke, Meatball, Terri and Billy laughed too.

From the corner of his hood, Duke watched as Brett stared hard into the gloom.

Another of Brett's friends tapped him on the shoulder. 'They're not here!' he hissed. 'Told you they wouldn't be. Come on.'

Brett gave a last glance over his shoulder, watching the rows of people who were now squealing with surprise.

Duke and the others sat still in their seats for several moments. It wasn't safe to move yet: Brett Tyler could still be around.

On the screen before them, the end credits started to roll, and the audience rose in little groups, chatting and laughing.

'We'll go out the front with everyone else,' Duke whispered. 'But keep a look out, just in case. Let's go.'

Billy and Terri got up and squeezed their way along to the edge of the seats.

'*Meatball* ...' Duke called back along the row. 'Meatball, come on!'

Still seated, Meatball gazed, unblinking, at the screen.

Terri walked along the row behind and leaned over. 'What is it?'

Meatball continued to stare at the screen, seemingly in a trance.

Terri shook him by the shoulder. 'Meatball!'

Snapping out of his trance, Meatball stood up, looking desperately worried. 'We've got problems,' he said.

'It's all right. Brett's gone.'

'Never mind him. Spike and the others are in trouble. We've got to get back to the station, quick.'

Duke looked at him. 'You've had another vision?'

Meatball nodded.

Back at the old railway station, Meatball stood in the empty waiting room looking around.

'Ok,' said Duke. 'Run over it again. Every bit of it. What exactly did you see?'

Meatball took a deep breath. 'Right. It was all on the screen back there at the cinema. I saw everything that happened to them after we left them here, like it was happening right in front of me. It's Spike and the others. They're in trouble.'

'But I thought they were headed ...'

'They didn't get the chance,' said Meatball. 'And now Gullivan's got them.'

'*Gullivan?*' Duke let out a long groan. 'I don't believe it. How?'

Meatball threw up his hands. 'I don't know, but he's definitely got them. And they're in this really strange place. One minute they're here, then they go through that door ...'

He pointed to the door leading to the platform on the opposite side.

'Why?' asked Billy.

Meatball shook his head, vaguely. 'Don't know that either,' he said. 'But wherever they are, it's night time ...'

'A time portal then,' Billy interrupted. 'It's got to be. It's the only explanation.'

Terri drew in a sharp breath. 'A time portal?'

Duke started. 'A time portal? But how?'

'Search me,' Meatball interrupted. 'I can't think of any other explanation either. One minute they're in the station waiting room, next thing they're in some kind of big room. And *he's* there. Gullivan. And it was definitely him, I'd know that skunk anywhere. Then he takes them outside and they're walking down a path.'

He broke off. 'I can see it again. It's like I said, it's dark. Outside this place, it's definitely dark.'

'Dark … as in night-time, you mean?'

'Yeah. They're walking down this path and he's behind them. Gullivan. He's behind them, pushing them in the back with his shotgun.'

Terri gasped. 'Oh *no* …'

'We've got to help them!' Billy yelled.

Duke grasped Meatball's arm. 'Meatball, where's he taking them, can you see? Where are they going?'

Meatball frowned, obviously trying to recall the image. 'There's some sort of big fort-type thing at the end of the path, with a fire and … there's people …'

'People? What sort of people?'

Meatball shook his head. 'I don't know. Just people. But sort of basic.'

'Basic?'

'Yeah, you know, like the things you see on telly. Not natives or nothing, but sort of like … basic clothes, you know, like …'

He suddenly snapped his fingers. 'You remember when we were learning about all that Roman stuff. You know, when they came over here, and all the local tribes and that?'

Billy gazed at him, mouth open. 'Romans?'

'Local tribes?'

'Yeah, you remember.'

Duke nodded, slowly. 'Yes, I think I know what you mean. You're right, they must've gone through a time portal. It's the only explanation.' He glanced back at Meatball. 'What happened after that?'

'He took them to this huge wooden place, like some kind of fort.'

'You mean a Roman stockade?' said Terri.

Meatball shrugged. 'Maybe ... yeah. Yeah, I suppose you could call it a stockade. Anyway, he's put them in there. Spike and the others. There's other people in there as well: soldiers of some sort. And thinking about it, they did look kind of like the ones in the books. But they weren't in charge.'

His face darkened. 'Gullivan's in charge. Least, that's the way it looked. And the other people were doing what he said.'

Terri grasped his arm. 'And Spike and the others? You definitely saw him put them inside?'

Meatball nodded. 'We've got to get them out.'

Duke ran his fingers through his hair. 'Oh no, of all the things to happen. First Tyler and now this. We've got to think,' he said. He looked around the waiting room at the peeling walls and paintwork, the thick dust covering the cracked plastic benches.

'Where did you say you saw the portal?'

'Over there,' said Billy. 'You said they went through that door.'

Meatball advanced towards the door on the opposite side of the waiting room. 'Yes. It was definitely through here.' He grasped the handle and then stopped and looked behind him. The other door was identical. 'Unless it was ...'

'Can't you remember?'

'I'm trying, I'm trying.' Meatball screwed his eyes shut in concentration. 'The green door ... the cream walls ... that's it!'

Meatball's eyes blinked open. 'The poster! They were looking at this poster - I don't know why - and then they

89

went through this door here.' He walked about, looking at things from different angles. 'Yes, I'm positive. It was this one.'

He gripped the handle. Taking a deep breath, he pulled it open and stepped straight out onto the opposite platform.

Billy rushed outside. Duke followed, staring around.

'This can't be it,' said Terri. 'We're still here!'

'It must be the other one then,' Meatball said, shaking his head, vaguely. 'But I could've sworn …'

He rushed to the opposite door. It led back onto the opposite platform.

'We can't get through!'

'We must be doing something *wrong*,' said Duke, trying to stay calm. 'There must be something else, something we're missing. Think, Meatball.'

'I *am* …'

'Hang on.' Terri eyes opened wide. 'You said something about a poster, didn't you?'

'You did!' Duke pointed. 'It must be this one here.'

Terri ran a hand slowly over the poster of the steam train. 'There *is* something. I can't make it out. There's a feeling in the middle here.'

As she spoke, the poster replayed its message, the steam train puffed out of the tunnel and the radiation sign appeared.

'What on earth?'

'It's a sign,' said Terri. 'It must be. A sign that the tunnel we found on the map is the right one. Spike must've seen it, realised what it was, and gone out of *that* door to avoid Brett.'

'Of course!' Duke ran across the room. 'Come on, let's try it again!'

They stumbled towards the door, jerked it open … and almost fell into Roman Britain.

CHAPTER FIFTEEN

Duke looked around. They were in a round room with wooden walls and very little light. 'Is this it?' he asked. 'The same surroundings you saw on the cinema screen?'

Meatball looked at it closely. 'Yeah, definitely. Wasn't expecting this smell though.'

Duke pulled a face. What a stench, he thought. Earth and timber and what smelled like paraffin and candles. And above all that, something else. Or was it some*one* else?

Terri coughed, holding a hand to her face. 'Oh, my goodness, it's awful.'

Duke hushed them both with a frantic wave of his hand. Now his eyes had become accustomed to the poor light, he'd noticed something over in the corner. A bed - if anyone could call it that - a ramshackle thing made up on the floor. A tatty, filthy quilt and a couple of old pillows that had probably been white once but were now dark brown with stains and other things he didn't want to think about.

Lying on top of this 'bed' in a disgusting, snoring, belching heap, was Cornelius Gullivan. He was the same colour as the bedding: filthy and grimy and reeking of sweat.

Beside him, on the earthen floor, were three bottles of rum, two empty and the third half full, with its contents leaking slowly out onto the mud. A shower of cigarette butts lay scattered where he'd ground them into the dirt.

Terri held her breath.

Meatball tapped Duke on the shoulder and began to mouth a silent message. 'Now what do we do?'

Billy yanked on Meatball's coat, pointing frantically to the wall beside the bed. They all recognised the thing propped against the timber. It was Gullivan's shotgun.

'If we can get that,' Billy was saying, silently, 'we'll be able to hold him off.'

Duke looked thoughtfully at Meatball and nodded. 'He's right.'

'I can get it!' Billy signalled, and before they could stop him, he was inching across the floor toward the gun. Duke groaned beneath his breath. One slip, one trip, and they'd all had it.

Billy was almost at the wall and just reaching out for the gun, when Gullivan stirred. They froze, holding their breath, mouths hanging open for fear that even closing them might wake him up.

With a loud snort and a belch, Gullivan's whole body turned over and settled in a curled position. Then he turned again, stretching out along the filthy quilt and sending an arm flailing across the pillow, releasing a cloud of sweaty aroma that wafted in their direction.

They waited, rigid, until his breathing settled once more into a monotonous, steady rhythm and his body relaxed and then Billy started again, Duke following close behind. Shotguns were heavy and if Billy dropped it, they were in trouble.

Gently, slowly, Billy reached out, slipped a hand around the gun, and lifted. He struggled for a moment as if it was heavier than he'd expected, but he managed to pass it to Duke, who swapped it to his other hand and, grasping Billy's coat, pulled him cautiously away.

'We have to get out,' Duke mouthed. 'Chance it. See if there's somewhere we can hide.'

Meatball nodded.

Terri suddenly grasped Duke's sleeve. 'I've spoken to Neeza!'

'*Neeza!*' Duke nodded at Meatball. 'Then we're in the right place!'

Terri nodded and then pointed towards the wall. 'She says there's some woods nearby just outside the door. It'll give us some cover.'

Duke beckoned toward the opposite end of the room. Cut into the wall was a large wooden door, secured by fastenings top and bottom.

'Bolts. Gullivan, I expect. Come on.'

Moving stiffly, they shuffled towards the door. Duke kept his eyes on the deep breaths shuddering through Gullivan's body, and the rise and fall of his sweaty chest.

It seemed like an hour, but in a few short minutes they had edged their way across the space between the bed and the door and now stood tugging on the bolts, praying they could open them quietly. To their surprise, the bolts slid easily across and the door opened.

Cautiously, Duke peered around the edge. He'd been expecting the darkness, but strangely it still came as a surprise.

Clutching the shotgun, he stepped outside, followed by Billy, Terri, and Meatball who closed the door silently behind them. The small, well-trodden path was directly in front of them, but Neeza was right, over to the side was a wooded area: an area that might give them some cover while they figured out what to do. At that moment, putting some distance between themselves and Gullivan was just as important.

They walked carefully across the ground to the trees and crouched down in the cover of the trunks. For a few moments they tried to calm themselves, racking their brains for an idea.

Around them, the darkness was all enveloping: a dense blackness broken only by the brilliance of the stars and a full moon.

'Neeza says you have to go right down the end of this path,' Terri whispered.

Meatball looked about him. 'This is it. This is definitely it. She's right, they went down this path and then there's the stockade thing.'

'Right.' Lifting aside some branches, Duke peered cautiously outside. 'We'll keep going as far as we can through these trees. No point in showing ourselves before we have to.'

'How are we going to get in, though? Neeza says it's guarded.'

Meatball closed his eyes. 'There were a couple of guys outside, I think. Guards, I suppose.'

Desperately, Duke tried to think of something. It was all very well rushing through to this place, but now what?

'I don't see how we can get them out,' he said. 'Unless we wave this gun about.'

'That won't get us anywhere,' hissed Meatball. 'There might be loads of them. And guards are hardly going to hand them over on our say-so, are they?'

Duke leaned despondently against a tree trunk. 'No.'

'You're not thinking straight,' said Billy. 'You've got to think logical.'

'What d'you mean, Bill?'

Billy slid off his hood. It was warmer on this side of the time portal, nothing like the tropical conditions they'd experienced last time, but a kind of gentle warmth - maybe of late spring or early summer.

'Well, they won't hand them over if *we* ask them,' he said. 'Not to us.'

He looked at Duke.

'But they will to *Gullivan*, won't they?'

'But he's out cold.'

'I know,' said Billy, 'so you could change into him and no one would ever know. You can go down there as Gullivan and get them to let Spike and the others out.'

Terri gasped. 'That might work! You can morph, can't you, Duke? Couldn't you morph into Gullivan?'

'You know, it might just work,' said Meatball, still cradling the shotgun over his shoulder. 'They won't know you're not Gullivan. You can stroll down there with this.' He patted the shotgun. 'And order them to let Spike and the others out.'

'Me?' Duke's heart started beating even harder. Walk down there, just like that?

He swallowed hard. What the others were saying was true, it *was* obvious, and he couldn't think of any other way.

'*May*be,' Terri began, gently, 'Maybe that's why you've got it now, Duke. Your special skill. Maybe you need to use it now.'

Seeing the look on Duke's face, she tailed off. 'Course, it's all very well suggesting it, I know, but it's going to take incredible courage. And there might be some other way,' she said. 'I'm going to contact Neeza again and see if they can think of something.'

Billy nodded. 'I think that might be a good idea.'

'No.' Duke tried to swallow the lump in his throat. 'No, don't do that. You're right. It's just, well …'

'We get it if you don't want to do it, mate,' Meatball said. 'I mean, it isn't going to be easy.'

Duke tried desperately to still his thumping heart. 'It's the only way, though. But I'm just wondering, I mean, what if he wakes up? There'll be two of us.'

'Looking at the state of him, I shouldn't think he'll be awake for ages,' Meatball remarked.

'The stockade's on the other side of these woods,' said Terri. 'Neeza says the woods were at their right hand side all the way along as Gullivan marched them down the path. I've told her what we might do, and they think it's a good idea. Spike thinks the rest of us can probably be close by in the woodland and not be detected.'

'Right.' Duke felt physically sick. 'I'll do it somehow,' he said, nervously. 'I'll have to. Though I don't know if I can change into Gullivan. I've only done this morphing thing a few times.'

Even as he was saying it, part of him was wishing he wouldn't have to do it. The other part of him felt guilty, especially as he knew if any of the others had this gift they would do it for him.

'Course we would,' said Terri, suddenly, as if she could read his thoughts, 'but that doesn't mean we wouldn't be terrified.'

Duke stood up on legs that felt like lead and then taking a deep breath, he closed his eyes. Through a shimmering blur, he became Cornelius Gullivan, from the tip of his filthy hair to the bottom of the heavy scuffed boots he always wore.

Turning his large, grimy head, he gazed at Meatball, who gazed back in admiration.

'Well?' he growled.

'Oh God, that's incredible,' Terri whispered. 'If I didn't know it was you …'

'Spot on,' said Meatball.

'The voice?'

'Perfect,' said Billy. 'You've got it, Duke. You're brilliant.'

Duke took another deep breath to steady his nerves. 'Right,' he croaked. 'Now what?'

Meatball passed over the shotgun. 'You're going to need this. From what I've seen there's only two guards. They've got swords, though, probably from the Romans. And don't forget there's soldiers inside too.'

'And it's dark 'n' all,' said Billy. 'But that's good. They won't be able to see you that clearly.'

'There's fires though,' Meatball went on, 'one inside and one nearby. And there's a couple of torch things by the gate.'

'Yeah, that's all great,' Duke growled. 'But how the hell do I get them to release Spike and the others?'

Terri grasped Meatball's arm. 'Think, Meatball, what did you see when he marched them down there? What did you see in your vision?'

Meatball lowered his eyes to stare at the ground, trying to remember. 'I saw Gullivan pushing them through the door and closing it behind and then he shoved them down the path in front of him. He's got this gun stuck in Spike's back so when you leave, make sure you do that till you're out of sight.'

He looked back down, as if he could see it on the ground. 'They're walking in front of him,' he said. 'They're at the stockade now and the guards on the gate are watching, but not moving. Gullivan's signalling them to open the door.'

'How?'

'He's waving his arm like this ...'

He swept an arm through the air. 'And they seem to know what it means, because they're opening the front gate.'

He stopped. 'Then there's the soldiers,' he said. 'Can't tell how many. And ...'

'And what?'

'I've just noticed,' he said. 'There's what's left of a couple more stuck on stakes, so be prepared for that.'

Duke nodded. If he was going to do this, that was the least of his worries.

'You'll be fine, Duke,' Billy urged. 'Inside you'll be you, but on the outside, you'll be Gullivan. He's quite a big bloke and nasty-looking and they seem to be scared of him.'

'I wish I knew why,' said Terri. 'He must have some sort of hold over them. Neeza says they treat him like a God.'

Duke felt queasy again. 'Let's hope this works. We haven't got much time.'

He looked back at the wooden enclosure where he hoped a snoring, belching Gullivan still lay in a drunken stupor. 'What if he wakes up?'

'We'll sort it,' said Meatball. 'I don't know how yet, but we'll think of something. Good luck, mate.'

Terri gave Duke a hug.

'Remember you're Gullivan,' hissed Billy. 'You're the boss. And you've got the gun.'

Duke nodded then, trembling with nerves, he stepped out of the woodland onto the path and, with a last glance behind, walked off toward the stockade.

CHAPTER SIXTEEN

In the dense woodland beside the path, Meatball, Terri and Billy pushed through the trees and bushes, trying to keep Duke in sight but fear for his safety constricting their breathing like an elastic band.

Striding down the beaten track, and struggling to walk casually with a large and cumbersome body, Duke was vaguely aware of their presence, and it comforted him.

The road ahead was in total darkness, but in the distance, he could see the flickering glow of firelight and clouds of smoke billowing into the night sky.

He marched on. His great long legs were obviously moving because his body was, but he could barely feel them. Just a numbness: a sort of floating sensation.

Heart in his mouth, he rounded the corner and there it was. The stockade. Larger than he'd imagined, but as Meatball had said, hardly qualifying as a stockade. It was simply a square prison of broad hewn trunks placed together and thrust into the ground like a barricade. Two men stood at the entrance. Behind them, lighted flares burned with a steady flame, and strong sulphurous fumes filled the air.

The men looked at him, expectantly.

Allowing himself a moment to steady his nerves, Duke steeled himself. It was now or never.

Taking one last deep breath, he stretched up to look as tall as he possibly could, balanced the shotgun against his shoulder, and approached the stockade. The two men straightened at once.

Fear lodged in Duke's throat as though someone was squeezing his windpipe. His mouth went dry.

What was the power Gullivan held over these people? There must be lots of them and only one of him.

Duke banished the thoughts from his mind. He needed to concentrate. He might look like Gullivan, he might smell like him, but if he didn't act like him it might be noticed.

The two men stared at him, waiting. Gullivan wouldn't hesitate, Duke thought, if he knew he had the advantage, he wouldn't hesitate.

Taking a step toward them, Duke lost his control over the long, muscled legs for only a second, and stumbled.

The men jumped to attention. Duke stared at them: at their fearful reaction. Of course, Gullivan was probably drunk more than he was sober. He was not a nice man at the best of times, but when he was drunk, he was terrifying.

Duke's heart pounded. With a pronounced slap on the gun, he moved it to his other hand and then, with an indistinct growl, he waved his free arm as Meatball had shown him.

The men rushed to open the gates. Behind them, Duke nearly collapsed with relief.

The large timber gates swung wide open and the two men stepped just inside.

Faced with the dim gloom beyond the opening, Duke suddenly realised he was completely unprepared for his next step. What now? Would they bring the others out? Course not, he thought, they're not going to do that, are they? Don't be stupid, how do they know what you want?

Perhaps he should just walk in. Oh hell, what if they shut the gate behind him?

Duke struggled to remain calm.

Don't be an idiot, he told himself. Chill. You're doing fine. You're Gullivan now and Spike knows you're coming, he knows you're coming …

In that instant, he knew he must get them to come outside.

Taking a deep breath, he gave an enormous belch, and began. 'All right, you revolting little brats!' he roared. 'Get out here!

There was a short pause, and then very gradually, Spike and the others appeared in the doorway, looking suspicious and wary.

Duke stepped towards them. 'Get out here!' he growled. 'I got plans for you lot!'

Nervously, they walked out through the opening, Jophan leading, Doc behind, and then Neeza, and Spike at the rear. Duke's heart lifted and pounded at the same time. It was going to work. It was going to work. He and Spike exchanged significant stares.

'Keep your mouth shut, boy, or you'll be sorry,' Duke snapped.

Jabbing the shotgun into Spike's back, he ordered them forward. 'Get up that path,' he snapped, viciously.

He cast a glance back at the two men, who rushed to close the gates and take up their positions.

Walking back up the path, Duke felt ten stone heavier. His legs felt so heavy that every step, every movement seemed painfully slow and laborious. He mustn't rush. He *couldn't* rush even if he tried. The path seemed suddenly longer. What if those men were behind him? He mustn't look back, Gullivan wouldn't look back.

Almost there … not yet … not yet …

They were nearly at the timber house before Duke allowed himself a glance back down the path. Tears pricked at his eyes as he realised it was gloriously empty. With another quick look, they slipped quietly into the wooded area where a relieved Meatball, Terri, and Billy were waiting to greet them.

'Oh my God, Duke, you were brilliant, brilliant, *brilliant!*' Terri hissed, as Duke melded back to his normal self, almost crying with relief.

She rushed to Spike and the others.

'You so were,' Meatball whispered. 'Amazing. Absolutely incredible!'

'Thanks, mate. I don't know what to say,' Spike mumbled. He thumped Duke on the shoulder. 'You've got some guts. I couldn't think how we were going to get out of there.'

'Your courage is an inspiration to us all,' said Jophan.

Billy stood by Spike, who looked down at him, and then squeezed his shoulder. 'It's ok,' he said, quietly. 'We're ok.'

Doc wiped tears from her face. 'Thank you, Duke,' she said. 'I am so glad to be out of there.'

She hugged him. Duke hugged her back, still hovering between laughter and tears. 'We all do stuff,' he said, generously. 'It was Bill's idea. And Meatball's vision.'

Neeza looked up at Jophan. His arm was about her shoulder. 'I am so relieved to see you all again,' she said, softly.

And us,' said Terri. She looked at the makeshift home where hopefully Gullivan still lay, snoring. 'There's still him. Somehow we've got to get past him.'

'If we could just see through that wall,' said Meatball. Spike nodded. 'We'll have to chance it.'

Thankfully, Gullivan was still snoring like a pig as they eased open the door and crept quietly back past his bed.

As carefully as he could, Duke put the gun back.

It was difficult to breathe in the saturated air inside, now heavy with fumes and the smell of alcohol, and they were little more than halfway across the musty floor, when Gullivan stirred.

Duke held his breath, his heartbeat rushing in his ears. Snorting, Gullivan rolled over onto his side. They waited until he started to snore, and then moved on.

'If he wakes, run for the portal,' Meatball whispered.

He'd barely closed his mouth when Gullivan gave a loud cry and sat up, sweat pricking on his face. Stunned, they stared at him, eyes wide. Bleary and stinking of sweat, Gullivan's head swayed about for a moment as he struggled to open his eyes and bring them into focus.

Silently, he continued to gaze at them as if trying to remember who they were. His mouth opened and then closed again.

No one moved or spoke. Terrified, they stood rooted to the spot, praying he was still in a drunken haze, and that he would just lie back down again.

Inside, Duke felt like screaming. Everything they'd just risked, all for nothing. Pretending to be Gullivan … facing those people …

Wait a minute, though. If he'd fooled the others, then maybe, just maybe …

In a sudden burst of inspiration, Duke changed shape again, to stand once more as Gullivan.

Now there were two Gullivans - both in the claustrophobic timber hut, but only the real one was awakening from a nightmarish hangover.

Through bloodshot, blinking eyes, the real Gullivan stared at Duke, trying desperately to focus. Duke scowled down at him and the real Gullivan found he'd awoken from one nightmare into another, looking straight at a copy of himself.

He sat limply on the edge of the bed, watching Duke. His jaw hung open, and he was scarcely able to believe his eyes. 'Who are you?' he croaked. 'How can ... no, no, it can't be …'

Sensing Gullivan's reaction, Duke started to walk slowly toward him, his eyes wide and staring and his face contorted into an evil grin.

Launching himself from the bed like a jack-in-the-box, Gullivan erupted into loud squeals of terror.

'N-o-o-o! N-o-o-o! Keep away from me-e …!'

His voice became a high-pitched shriek. Wailing and yelling, he threw himself against the wall, tearing and clawing at the door and scrambling frantically to undo the bolts. Then, with a powerful lunge, the door flew open and he crashed through it and out into the night.

The second he'd disappeared from view, they turned and ran, bursting back through the portal, one by one, and into the station waiting room.

Falling onto the seats, they looked at each other.

'It worked,' said Duke. 'I can't believe it. It actually worked.'

Meatball closed his eyes. 'That could've gone *so* wrong.'

'Don't think about it,' Spike said. 'It didn't.' He looked around him. 'Thank God we're back.'

He broke off to look at Duke, who was slowly resuming his real shape. 'Wish I knew how you did that, Duke.'

'Me, too,' Duke croaked. 'I'm just lucky it's me that can do it ... I *think*.'

Everyone started to laugh, before they cried.

'The face of Cornelius Gullivan.' Jophan chuckled. 'That is a memory I shall treasure.'

Billy got to his feet. 'We need to carry on, though. We've lost loads of time already and we've still got to find the tunnel.'

'Billy is correct,' said Jophan. 'The tunnel and our mission are of paramount importance. We must continue.'

'Oh, my goodness, the crystal!' Terri cried. 'We forgot about the crystal! Neeza, do you still have it?'

Smiling, Neeza reached into her coat and retrieved the golden chain. The purple crystal hung safely in the centre.

'It is still with me,' she said.

'Thank heavens Gullivan didn't see it,' Spike said. 'If he'd clapped eyes on it ...'

'Yeah, well, he didn't,' Meatball said, gruffly. 'Anyway, we haven't got time to talk about everything now. We need to find this tunnel.'

Duke delved into his coat pocket and pulled out the map. 'This has got to be the one,' he said. 'I can't see it can be anywhere else. And then there's the poster. It's got to be the right one, hasn't it?'

Spike nodded. 'Must be. And at some point, it seems to run straight through Temperance Hill.'

Duke glanced out through the window. It seemed strange to see snowflakes when so recently it had been mild and warm, but snowflakes there were, torrents of them - thick and fluffy and tumbling down across the countryside covering everything like a quilt.

Pulling their coats and scarves tightly around them, they stepped through the door onto the platform and jumped down into the old railway cutting.

There were no longer any rails or trains to keep nature in check and over the years plants, bushes, and trees had seeded themselves along the sloping banks. They were already heavy with snow, but the centre was still relatively clear, forming a narrow footpath.

For once, Duke was glad of the snow for a little extra light: the daylight was fading and the trees either side made it difficult to see clearly. Ahead of them, Temperance Hill loomed up out of the countryside, vast and unwelcoming.

'According to the map,' Duke said, spitting out a snowflake that had stuck to his lip, 'if we follow this cutting there should be a siding - a sort of spur coming off it somewhere, and that would've been the track that runs into the tunnel. The problem is finding it. The further we get along this track, the thicker the undergrowth is getting.'

They began to work their way systematically along the banks of the cutting, peering through the undergrowth.

'It is here!'

They looked up. Neeza was some distance ahead, at the side of the cutting. Terri was beside her, tugging at some large branches.

'It's here!' she called. 'Behind this lot! It's over here! Quick!'

The others stomped through the snow to the spot and peered through. Beyond a barrier of tangled branches, it was possible to make out the banks of the siding, now considerably overgrown.

'This has got to be it,' Spike said, craning his neck to see into the distance. 'It must run off towards the hill.'

The branches were sharp and rough, matted with coarse grasses and the dead remains of wild flowers. Showers of snow catapulted into their faces as they dragged their way through.

After a struggle, they finally stepped through into the siding. Here, too, the steep sides were overgrown, but through the centre there was still a narrow path. For some distance, it curved off around a corner and the banks grew steadily steeper. Temperance Hill was just visible through a gap in the trees.

'We must be getting nearer,' Doc puffed, as the path ran deeper between the banks. 'Look how high the sides are here: we must be heading underground soon.'

'So where's the tunnel?' Billy asked. 'There should be a tunnel here somewhere.'

At that moment, the path ended. And there it was in front of them: an enormous brick tunnel, now completely overgrown. Across the entrance stretched a vast holly bush, laden with snow, its thick branches forming a dimpled cushion of white. Patches of dark green and red peeped through where the snow had fallen to the ground.

Weaving around the holly, in and out of the huge gnarled base, through the branches, over the sides of the tunnel and up over the keystone, was an enormous ivy, its cupped leaves laced with snow.

Steadily, they gazed at it.

'It looks like a Christmas card,' Terri breathed.

Billy let out a yell. '*The Christmas card!*'

CHAPTER SEVENTEEN

Billy's chilled face broke into a smile. 'The words in the Christmas card! That was something about holly and ivy!'

Hurriedly unzipping his coat, Spike reached into his inside pocket, and read aloud the words on the crumpled Christmas card. '*The holly and the ivy, when they are both full grown.*'

'Well, that's them all right,' said Duke, staring at the huge holly blocking the tunnel entrance.

Spike read the rest of the verse. '*This should put you on the right track ...*'

'*If you've got tunnel vision,*' finished Meatball. 'I remember that bit.'

'Well, that's it, then,' said Doc. 'This has to be the right place: it's too much of a coincidence. Now all we have to do is shift this lot.'

'Don't think that's going to be too easy,' Duke said. 'Why didn't we think to bring an axe or something?'

'Because we didn't know we were going to need it. It was different before.'

'I, too, did not consider such a circumstance,' said Jophan. He leaned closer to the ivy to examine it. 'It appears firmly affixed to these surfaces.'

'D'you know,' Doc said, 'ivy actually excretes a sort of glue to fix itself ...' Her voice tailed away as they stared at her. 'Just saying.'

'Great, Doc.' Slipping his large hands beneath a mass of ivy, Meatball pulled at the stems. 'Let's see if we can unglue it.'

The stems scarcely moved.

'Pretty strong glue,' Billy said.

'Strongest things are always in nature,' Doc said, wistfully.

'Give it a rest, Doc,' Duke muttered. He tugged hard at the ivy, but it was clinging to the tunnel as if it was superglued.

'Sorry.' Doc tugged with all her might. 'I'm still a bit weird after that healing thingy.'

Meatball turned to look at her. 'Healing thingy? What healing thingy?'

Spike's eyes opened wide as he suddenly remembered. 'Oh *yeah*! With everything else going on, I forgot!'

'Doc has been blessed,' Neeza said, admiringly. 'She has been blessed with the gift of healing.'

Doc went a little pink. 'Well … er …'

'It was amazing,' Spike rushed on. 'You're never going to believe it.'

Everyone stopped pulling at the ivy and listened.

'There was a wounded soldier,' Jophan said. 'Badly wounded. A deep gash to his side. From a sword, we think. He was gravely ill and bleeding heavily.'

'And Doc *healed* him!' cried Spike. 'Right then and there, in front of us. She just knelt down, put her hands over him – you know, like you see on the telly – and then there was this kind of glowing, she said, and suddenly his wound was gone! Disappeared! And he opened his eyes and looked at us. And he said something to Doc, didn't he, Doc? What was it?'

'Angelus,' Doc murmured.

'Angel,' said Meatball. 'That's what that is. He thought you were an angel. And no wonder.'

Terri grabbed Doc's arm, and shook it. 'Oh *Doc* … wow!'

Sheepishly, Doc looked down at her hands. 'I don't know how it happened, though,' she said, glancing from one to the other of them. 'I don't even really remember doing it.'

'You were incredible,' Neeza said. 'It is a gift I could wish to possess.'

'It was indeed a miracle,' said Jophan.

107

Billy sighed. 'Wish I'd seen it.'

'Guess that must be your skill then, Doc,' said Meatball, shaking his head in amazement.

'Looks like it,' said Duke. 'And I thought mine was incredible.'

'Yours is incredible,' Spike said, longingly. 'They're all incredible.'

Terri looked at him. 'Yours'll turn up.'

Really, he thought? Like when?

Feeling annoyed and frustrated, he grasped a large section of ivy and yanked on it. With a loud ripping sound, it tore from the tunnel wall, sending several thick branches, and Spike, flying backwards into the snow.

'How did you do that?'

Climbing to his feet, Spike shrugged. 'Just pulled it,' he said. 'Like this.'

He grabbed a thick branch of holly and tugged. The whole bush bent towards him amid sounds of scraping brickwork. Slightly alarmed, he let it slip from his fingers and spring back.

'Wow, what have you been eating?'

Trying to hide the fact that he was slightly startled, Spike frowned. 'Stop mucking about,' he said. 'Come on, give me a hand with this.'

He reached again for the holly trunk, pulled at it, and watched in amazement as the whole tree lifted, roots and all, clean out of the ground. With it came long whipping vines of ivy and several lumps of masonry from the tunnel entrance, shrouded in a cloud of dust.

The others dived for cover.

Choking in the dust and debris, they watched, incredulous, as the whole holly tree flew from his grasp and landed several feet away up the bank behind them, crushing the undergrowth and sending showers of snow tumbling to the ground.

'Oh, my *goodness* …'

Mouth hanging open, Spike held out his arms, turning his hands repeatedly over and back again. Had he just done that? How?

Leaning across, Billy prodded Spike's hand with his finger. 'Ok, how did you do that?'

Spike didn't answer. Completely bewildered, he continued to stare at his hands. They didn't even hurt!

'Wow, mate.'

'I'm not even going to ask what you had for breakfast,' Duke said.

'Told you.' Terri giggled. 'Told you it wouldn't be long.'

Spike let out a cry. 'Hells bells and buckets of blood!'

'What?'

'It's something Mr Price says.' Then he started to laugh. A vision of Brett Tyler appeared in his mind. Wow, was this strength thing ever going to be cool.

'Well, however you did it, you can have a go at this next,' said Meatball, examining the tunnel entrance. 'The whole thing's been bricked up by the look of it.' Lifting his booted foot, he kicked at the brickwork with little result. 'And it isn't moving anytime soon.'

Spike approached the brick wall and looked it up and down. 'Don't know about this,' he said. 'What happens if the whole tunnel comes down?'

'You don't *kick* it,' Doc tutted, running a hand over the bricks. 'But with your strength, you might be able to pull them out - you know, one by one. Start with this one here, look, near the top. Looks as if this might work loose with a knife or something. Then once you've got one loose ...'

Billy dipped into his pocket. 'I've got my penknife. Will this do?'

Spike took the knife from Billy's hand and grasped the blade. It bent like butter.

'Sorry,' he said, straightening it. 'Don't know my own strength.'

He began scraping at the mortar between the bricks until it crumbled sufficiently to allow his fingers in through the gap.

Taking a firm grasp, he tugged on a brick. It crumbled to dust in his hands.

'Oops,' he said.

He tucked a hand in and slid out the remaining bricks: some in pieces, some in a crumble of dust, and kept removing them until there was an entrance large enough to walk through.

'Looks a bit creepy,' said Terri, peering into the gloom. 'There could be anything in there.'

She turned to Neeza. 'You said something about the crystal lighting our way?'

Neeza nodded, the crystal already in her hand.

'It must be the right place,' Duke said. 'But we've got a long walk till we get to the Manor, so I hope you're right.'

'Here, what's the time?'

Spike glanced at his watch. 'It's half three already!'

'Half three? It can't be!'

'Come on, quick,' said Duke. 'Let's get going. We can't afford to waste any more time.'

Grasping the side of the bricks, he stepped inside the tunnel. The others followed. As Neeza stepped into the darkness, the crystal blossomed with light, forming an arc of radiance up the walls and across the ceiling that travelled with them down the tunnel as they walked.

'Thank goodness,' said Duke. He looked back. 'Watch yourself, there's still rails on this bit.'

Stepping carefully alongside the rails, they followed the tunnel as it veered off around a corner.

At the bend, Spike glanced back over his shoulder. The light flooding in the opening had slowly diminished and was now a small white shape in the distance. The darkness didn't bother him, Neeza had said the crystal would be enough, and it was, but deep down, he felt a little disturbed at being in such an enclosed space.

In the purple light, he glanced across at Jophan, who looked just as uneasy. Maybe he's not used to this sort of stuff, he thought. It must all be really weird for them.

'Bit dark in here, isn't it?'

Jophan looked back at him and nodded. 'When Father mentioned assisting you all in this task, it seemed so exciting,' he said. 'Such a wonderful adventure. But now ...'

'Don't worry about it, mate,' Meatball whispered. 'You're not the only one. Right now, I want to run out of this place.'

'And I,' said Jophan. 'But I must protect Neeza. Father would expect no less.'

'We're all in this together,' said Spike. 'We protect each other.'

'There's something ahead!' called Billy. 'A sign or something.'

They increased their pace. Over on the wall an old sign appeared in the light of the crystal. Originally a bright cream, but now rusted and mellowed to a dull brown, the blue letters were still clear.

'*No unauthorised personnel beyond this point,*' read Meatball. 'Then we must be in the right place.'

'And hopefully it's not too much further ahead,' said Terri. 'Thank God. I hate tunnels.'

'Me 'n' all,' said Duke. 'This place is starting to give me the creeps.'

'Let's speed it up a bit,' Meatball said. 'I know it's impossible, but I keep thinking some train's going to rush round the corner out of the dark.'

They walked on. Spike was glad of the light pouring from the crystal, but desperate for any sign of an end to the tunnel.

He glanced up. Above, on the curving roof, strange white calcified growths hung down, water dripping from them at intervals, and running in small rivulets down the brick walls.

Large spider's webs, coated in dust, draped like delicate lace curtains between the roof and sides, and here and there, long fibrous roots pierced the roof, grasping at the bricks like bony, luminous fingers.

As the light splayed across, insects scattered in all directions.

Shuddering, Terri pulled her collar tightly around her neck whilst trying to watch all around her. 'Please let this tunnel end soon,' she wailed.

'Can't be much longer,' Doc said.

They continued, the tunnel stretching into the distance. The light from the crystal blazed the way, but as the darkness closed in behind them, it was beginning to feel as though the walls and roof were coming in.

'Surely, we must be near it,' said Spike. 'We've been walking ages.'

The tunnel started to curve once more. Suddenly they were on a slope: a slope of smooth concrete that led up onto a long platform. Beyond the end of that platform, a set of huge buffers signalled the end of the line.

'We are here,' said Jophan, with obvious relief.

In the light of the crystal, they looked about them. Set into the wall behind and spreading from one side of the platform to the other was a large arch. With dismay, they realised it was both a beginning and an end. Completely filled in, it had only a heavy metal door let into the base, with a thick rusted handle halfway down its length.

'This has got to be it,' Meatball said, approaching the door. He put out a hand to grasp the handle, and as he touched it the outer frame of the door pulsed with a deep purple light.

'It *is*!' Doc yelled. 'This *is* the way!'

Gripping the handle, Meatball pushed down the lever and pulled as hard as he could.

'I can't budge it!' he groaned. 'Here, Spike, you'd better have a go.'

Spike stepped forward, took a deep breath, and took hold of the handle. Pressing down with all his might, he pulled and pulled and then slipped both hands around and tried again. The door rocked in its frame but refused to open.

'There's something there,' he said, pulling on it again, 'something on the inside holding it closed. Bolts or something. Top and bottom by the feel of it. They must be rusted in.'

He tried to peer down the edge of the door, but it was hopeless.

'This is ridiculous,' Terri said. 'We've come all this way and now we can't open the door? We must be able to: why would it have glowed purple if it isn't the right door?'

'Oh hell!' snapped Duke. 'Could this be any more difficult?'

'I've got an idea,' said Billy. The others turned to look at him. 'D'you remember about the discs in the spaceship? Jophan and Neeza said they were taught to focus their minds when they were young.'

Spike shook his head. 'And?'

'Well, if they can do that, then maybe they can move the bolts the same way.'

'I see.' Jophan's eyes opened wide. 'Yes, I see. You are correct, Billy, it may be possible.' He walked forward. 'I will try.'

Placing both hands on the door, he closed his eyes and began to concentrate. After a long silence, they could just make out a slight scraping sound on the other side of the door.

'It is difficult,' Jophan said, gasping. 'The bolts are heavy and do not move freely.'

'We must join together,' said Neeza, gently. 'We are stronger together.'

She put her hands next to his on the door and closed her eyes. The door began to vibrate.

Slight scraping sounds could be heard, followed by a soft, slow sliding noise.

'It is done,' said Jophan.

He pushed down on the handle, and with Spike's help, they dragged it open, and stared inside.

The corridor was dimly lit, narrower with a low ceiling and the walls and floor were tiled and glossy. Carefully, they stepped in and closed the door behind them.

'It's like an old Underground station.'

They shuffled quietly along, following as it curved around a corner into a long, straight corridor.

At the end, a second corridor ran across the top like a T-junction. Which way now?

'There!' hissed Duke, pointing to the left. 'That door! It glowed purple!

Another sign glowed on the door. '*Maintenance and Access Shaft. Authorised Personnel Only.*'

'There's a lock,' said Spike, inspecting the door. 'One of those number-coded things.'

'I've got that.' Terri closed her eyes. Gus' memories reappeared in her mind.

'6,' she said. '8 … 3 … 9 … 9,2,4 …7.'

Spike tapped in the numbers and turned the handle. It clicked open.

Slipping in through the door, they found themselves in a large square space of shimmering metal. In the centre, a huge metal tube stretched down through the floor with spiralling stairs running around the sides.

They glanced around the walls, searching for something, anything, that might show them the way.

'Nothing,' Duke said. 'Maybe …'

Moving across to the spiral staircase, he peered down to the floor below. 'Let's try down here!'

Treading silently, they slipped down the steps, and into a slightly narrower space, studded with silver-coloured pipes running in all directions.

'Now what?'

Neeza looked down at the crystal, which had begun to pulse steadily. 'We're very near, we have to be.'

A purple flash seemed to leap from a square opening near the bottom of the wall.

Meatball stepped nearer and leaned down. 'Here, look! This just flashed purple. This must be it.'

Spike stared at the opening on the wall. Small, and lined with gleaming metal, it looked nowhere near large enough to accommodate any of them.

Terri peered inside the shaft. 'It's the one all right,' she said. 'The whole corridor's pulsing purple inside. Look.'

They crouched down to study it.

'Well, that's it, then. It's got to be the right place.'

'Perhaps we can just push the crystal in,' Duke said.

Neeza shook her head. 'No. It has to be placed in position in the shaft,' she said. 'Remember Father said we would have to make our way back down the shaft.'

Spike gaped. 'We? I can't possibly get in *that* ... Bill?'

Billy slid an arm and a small area of his shoulder into the shaft. 'No way,' he said. 'I can't get in that space. I'll get stuck.'

'It is too narrow,' Jophan interrupted, peering into it. 'I cannot possibly fit.'

Meatball glanced at the opening. 'Well, don't look at me.'

'I can.'

Doc was smiling. 'I can do it,' she said, brightly. 'I'm quite small. I think if I lie full length, I can slide along it.'

'I, also,' said Neeza, who was the same slender build. 'Doc and I shall do it.'

'But ...'

'It's the only way,' Doc said, casually, with a look that said she wished she'd kept her ideas to herself. She gave a nervous laugh.

'I shall go first, with the crystal,' said Neeza.

'Ok, I'll be right behind you. Let's just hope we can reach far enough.'

Neeza picked up the crystal and looked at it, and then she carefully slipped it from the chain and gripped it tightly.

'We have no option,' she said. 'We cannot fail.'

CHAPTER EIGHTEEN

In the close, sterile room at the bottom of the staircase, Meatball stared down the small opening in the wall. The hard surface of the metal sides stretched away into the distance as far as he could see, sleek and smooth and unwelcoming like a gleaming silver cage.

'Please God,' he murmured. 'Don't let it be too far down that thing.'

Beside him, Neeza held tightly onto the crystal and took a long, deep breath. 'We must begin at once. We have not much time.'

Spike glanced at his watch. 'Hell! It's just gone four! Somehow, we've got to get the crystal in the right place and get out again by half past!'

'Then let's get on with it.'

Bending forward, Neeza slid her head and shoulders carefully into the shaft. 'It is tight,' she said. 'There is little room for movement, but it is possible.'

She shuffled further in.

Doc waited until her feet disappeared inside the shaft and then prepared to follow.

'Are you all right, Neez?'

'Yes.' Her voice echoed down the shaft. 'There is sufficient room, Doc. I am sliding a little further down.'

'Not too far. Wait for me.' Crouching down, Doc slid her head and shoulders into the opening. 'It's a tight fit,' she called. 'There's barely enough room to move along. Ok, let's get going.'

'Don't go on if it gets too narrow,' Duke said. 'We'll think of something else.'

Something else, Spike thought? By half past?

'Keep calling down the shaft as you go,' said Billy. 'We'll be able to hear you.'

'I will. Neeza's just ahead. She's watching for me.'

Spike watched anxiously as Doc's feet disappeared. 'Keep calling,' he said. 'Both of you.'

He stood with the others, listening to the sounds of sliding, squeaking hands and knees echoing down the walls of the shaft. If we're going to pray, he thought, now's a good time. What if Doc and Neeza got stuck inside that thing? How could they possibly rescue them?

Duke bent to call into the shaft. 'Keep talking! Can you see how far it is?'

'We cannot as yet see the end.' Neeza's voice was slightly fainter. 'It stretches away into the distance.'

Jophan pushed Duke aside. 'Are you safe?'

'We're fine, Jo,' Doc called. Her voice sounded weak and strained with panic.

'I thought the tunnel was bad enough,' Meatball said. 'Goodness knows what it's like in there.'

'I don't want to think about it,' said Terri.

Billy peered into the opening. 'It must be really hot too.'

'Anything, yet?' Jophan called.

'No,' called Doc. 'Anything, Neez?'

Her reply was faint. 'Nothing as yet. The crystal will let us know.'

A few moments later, they heard Doc's voice. 'Is the crystal doing anything yet?'

'No,' came the echo. 'It still pulses. But I do hope it is not much further.'

'Me too,' said Doc.

'Are you both ok?' Terri called into the opening, then stood up. 'They can't hear us,' she said. 'I can't stand this. I'll try contacting Neez.'

She closed her eyes for a moment, while Jophan watched her, anxiously.

'Are they all right?' Duke asked.

Terri took a deep breath and nodded. 'She says they're ok, quite a way down already, but nothing's happening with the crystal yet.'

'It's supposed to go white, isn't it?'

'Father said they will know when it is time,' said Jophan.

'Well, I wish it would hurry up,' Duke said. 'Are they ok, Terri?'

Terri stared at them, helplessly. 'It's gone,' she said. 'I can't hear her.'

'*What*!'

'I'm trying,' she said. 'But I can't hear her.'

Rushing across to the shaft, Jophan peered in, cupping his hands. 'NEEZA! DOC!'

Duke leaned forward and banged on the metal wall. 'DOC!'

'Don't do that!' said Meatball. 'You'll deafen them!'

'What's the time now?'

Spike glanced at his watch. 'Three minutes later than the last time you asked me, Bill,' he snapped. 'Almost ten past. For goodness sake, how much longer?'

'I … I still can't reach her!' Terri's voice was rising with panic. 'I can't reach her!'

Desperately crowding around the opening of the shaft, they struggled to shout into the same space.

'DOC! NEEZA! Answer, for goodness sake!'

'SAY SOMETHING!'

'D-O-C!!'

At that moment, as if borne on a gust of wind, they heard Doc's voice, faint and distant. It was a hollow cry as though she was at the bottom of a well.

'Something's happened!'

Terri suddenly let out a cry of joy. 'No! No, it's all right, I've got her! I can hear Neeza again! She says the crystal's in place and they're on their way back!'

Duke and Meatball punched the air. 'Yes!'

'Brilliant!' yelled Spike and Billy together.

Jophan stood with Terri, staring at her expectantly. 'They are returning?'

With a deep sigh, she nodded at him, smiling. 'Yes, Jo, they're on their way back.'

His head fell forward as a wave of relief washed over him. 'Neez says it's more difficult coming backwards, but they're going as fast as they can.' Terri looked across at Spike. 'They're asking me how we are for time.'

'Tell them we're ok for time,' Billy said. 'Or they might start panicking.'

Spike glanced at his watch. 'I wish I could. It's gone twenty-past.'

Duke bent to peer into the opening, ready to grab Doc's ankles the second she was within reach.

'Where are they? It's twenty-four minutes past …'

'They're coming,' Terri said. 'It's not so easy coming out backwards.'

Hearts pounding, they waited, as time passed like a whisper on the air.

'There!'

Duke yelled out and reached in with his arm. Pushing hard against the wall, he stretched out his fingertips. 'I've got her! I've got her ankle!'

With an enormous pull, Doc flew from the opening like a cork from a bottle, followed by Neeza, scooped up by Jophan as she slid toward the floor.

'Thank goodness you're both all right!'

'It's nearly half past!' Spike yelled. 'Let's get out of here, quick!'

Spinning around, he took a step towards the door … and found himself lifted off his feet and into the air.

In that instant, everything changed to the languid, slow motion drifting of a space flight.

Captured in the same yawning time lapse that had so efficiently delayed Brett Tyler and his gang, they floated weightlessly through syrupy air, arms and legs drifting in all directions. Tumbling around like clothes in a dryer, they suddenly found themselves lifted and held gently but firmly against the wall, their feet dangling in mid-air.

Gradually lifting his head, Spike stared at the wall they'd left behind, at the opening where the girls had entered and where now a purple light was rolling down the shaft in a thick glowing wave.

On it came, shimmering and swirling and spilling forward out of the end of the shaft. Pouring into the room in a crescendo of light, it soared upwards and outwards, expanding at speed into an enormous sphere, with the outer perimeter stretching and stretching and advancing closer toward them.

It was impossible to move. Pressed hard against the wall by an unseen force, Spike closed his eyes and prayed. They weren't supposed to be here, they were supposed to be gone. Half past four, Arisius had said. Was this the end for all of them? Please, no ...

He felt the pressure of the expanding sphere, and the heat. Closer ... closer ...

Almost upon them, the sphere continued to swell like an enormous purple balloon, stretching, and straining until just a breath away from their faces, it stopped and set in position.

Gripped by shock and fascination, Spike watched events unfold like a disaster movie, frame by terrifying frame.

First the shaft was gone, then the wall was gone and then every structure, every fortification, every piece of construction between them and the reactor chamber, vanished. Nothing remained: nothing except the sphere and the swirling maelstrom within: a violent tornado of metal, concrete, and wood slowly and relentlessly being ripped apart and pulverised to dust.

Spike watched through half-closed eyes as the dust storm gathered momentum, the dust thickened and darkened, and then drained like an hourglass into the crystal beneath.

And then, suddenly, the dust was gone and through the outer skin they could see everything, and there it was, deep inside the sphere in front of them.

It was the thing that mattered, the reason for their mission and the thing that could destroy everything they knew and loved.

CHAPTER NINETEEN

'Is that the *reactor*?'

Billy whispered the words, breathing into the narrow, claustrophobic space between them and the wall of the purple sphere.

Spike had given no thought as to how the reactor might look: how big it might be, what colour or form it would take. Everyone had seen pictures of nuclear power stations and film of atomic explosions, but a reactor?

Watching it as it floated suspended inside the sphere, he realised none of them knew for certain whether this large innocuous looking metal cylinder actually *was* the reactor. All he knew about the reactor was that it was new, experimental, and capable of appalling devastation.

He stared at the cylinder. Ten feet or more in diameter and slightly less in height, it was studded with holes, all that remained of its connecting pipe work.

As he watched, the skin of the cylinder tinged dull red at the tips, the colour creeping slowly across the highly polished metal. Moments later, this had progressed to a deep red pulse. The red progressed to vivid orange, through yellow, and on into brilliant white.

Spike gawped. Being this close to it … seeing all this unfold in front of their eyes. And yet they were still alive … how was it possible?

He struggled to hold back a sob. What if it gave way? What if the sphere gave way and didn't protect them?

As the brilliance inside the sphere increased, the outer skin began to darken.

From the holes in the cylinder's surface, white-hot flares of gas exploded outwards, spewing like silver rain. The outer skin of the cylinder shimmered and then seemed to melt, trembling like simmering water. The sphere darkened and great globules of white-hot metal ran down its side.

Held fast against the wall of the room, they gazed in through the semi-transparent skin of the sphere, now darkening rapidly to protect their eyes.

'*Oh my God, this must be it ...*' Doc's voice was tremulous and vaguely distant. '*Help us ...*'

The sphere was black now: a solid impenetrable shroud of darkness, shielding them and protecting them from the annihilating heat, light and radiation inside.

They saw nothing more, but as events progressed inside, the outer surface of the sphere ballooned slightly. It was the only visible sign of the titanic pressure it held.

'It's getting *closer.*' Panic rose in Terri's voice. 'This bubble thing ... it's squeezing us. I can't breathe. It's ... it's so tight ...'

'Be still.' Jophan's voice was weak. 'All will be well. Father said so. *It must be ...*'

Somewhere deep inside, Spike's heart pounded violently. 'Yeah, but ...'

He stopped speaking as the tightness increased. But we were supposed to be well away from here, he wanted to say. We were supposed to be a safe distance away.

Beside him, he could see Terri shaking with fear. 'We're going to suffocate,' she wailed. 'We're going to suffocate!'

Meatball dragged in what he could of a breath. 'So much for my vision,' he said. 'So much for that woman, whoever she is. It looks like we've had it.'

Caught in the iron grip of the sphere, they waited desperately for the pressure to ease, but nothing happened. Time dragged on. In the room, there was absolute silence. Nothing moved. The sphere seemed frozen in position.

'Why has it stopped?' Duke's voice rose to a yell. 'Why has it stopped! Something's gone wrong!'

'I do not understand,' Neeza said, her voice feeble with emotion. 'Father said all would be well. It cannot stop now.'

Pulling in a breath, Spike held onto it for a moment. 'It's our fault,' he gasped. 'We were late. We should've been gone and none of this would've mattered.' A tear rolled down his cheek. *'None of this would've mattered …'*

'Spike …'

Spike's arm fought against the sphere, reaching desperately for any touch of Billy. Nothing, he thought miserably, there's nothing, and it was all their fault. They were going to die here, suffocating beneath this thing and they couldn't do a thing.

Frustration welled up within him as he pushed with all his might against the wall of the sphere. His super strength … where was it? What the hell use was it if he couldn't save them?

Panting, he laid back against the wall. The skin of the sphere immediately filled the void, folding in around him, pinning him fast. Please let this end, oh God, please let it end.

Time passed, and still they waited, pressed tightly against the wall, unable to move or speak. If only they could see …

Just then, the outer skin of the sphere began to ripple in soft tremors. The tremors became a rumble, and they closed their eyes as a kind of ghostly howl reverberated through their heads. The howl rose higher and higher to an ear-splitting shriek and then just when they felt they couldn't tolerate any more, the pressure suddenly released, leaving them gasping.

'Thank *God*,' Doc let out a sob. 'Thank God. It's easing.'

'It's clearing,' Duke croaked. 'The outside of the balloon. It's clearing again.'

Billy peered in through the outer wall. 'Look at it. It's like one of those snow-globes.' He watched eddies of swirling debris whipping around the sphere. 'Everything's been smashed to dust.'

As swiftly as it had begun, the swirling ceased and all was still. It was quiet for a time, then the outer skin of the sphere started to contract at speed, releasing its hold on them so swiftly they slid down the wall and landed on the hard floor in a heap.

They watched as the sphere moved rapidly across the room, shrinking like a deflating balloon, rebuilding the room as it went.

It began with the outer wall, constructing it in pixelating sections like a puzzle cube. Twisting and turning this way and that, it moved at lightning speed, before snapping into a solid mass.

The inner wall then started to rebuild itself from the outer edge toward the centre, shunting and sliding in large blocks, whipping violently around, repairing and replacing everything as it was.

As it moved toward the middle, it closed in, revealing the square shaft once more at its centre, and then with a snapping sound, the purple wave sucked back inside the shaft, rebuilding as it went. For a moment the shaft was a mass of sparks … and then it was over.

Stunned, they sat for a few moments where they'd dropped from the wall, a tangle of arms and legs, too dazed to move. Their heads were reeling, bodies aching from the constant pressure.

Finally, with some effort, Spike opened his mouth to speak. 'I'm not even going to ask what happened,' he said, weakly.

'Nor me,' groaned Meatball.

'What *happened?* What do you mean, what happened? A nuclear detonation,' Doc said. 'That's what happened. Somehow, we just sat through a nuclear detonation and we're still alive. But how? That reactor thing just went critical and we're still here to talk about it? In what reality?'

'I don't know,' said Duke. 'Only thing I know is I want to go home.'

'All is done,' said Jophan, quietly. 'The reactor is made safe. Everything is secure.'

The others looked at him.

'I do not know how I know this either,' he said. 'But I do.'

'I guess it must be,' Spike said, gruffly. 'Cause we're still here.'

Terri pushed herself unsteadily to her feet. 'Well, we know what we have to do now, don't we? We have to get the crystal back.'

'Yes,' said Neeza, nodding. 'That is our next task. Doc and …'

'I know,' Doc snapped, before she could finish. '*I know.*' She looked across at the wall that only moments before had been thundering around, rebuilding itself. 'How can it be solid again?' she said. 'How can the shaft still be in the same place? How can the crystal still be inside?'

Approaching the shaft, she leaned down to peer in. 'It looks exactly the same,' she said. Cautiously, she put out a hand to feel the inside wall. 'It's completely cold. All that movement, all those blocks sliding and turning, the sparks at the end … yet the shaft's completely cold …'

'I shall go first,' said Neeza, climbing into the shaft.

'Wait for me.' Doc clambered in after her.

The journey back through the shaft seemed easier without the added pressure of a time limit. Still calling to the others waiting patiently in the reactor room, they slid carefully along in swift, rhythmic movements. Suddenly, just ahead, Neeza glimpsed the crystal, in the same place, still and silent.

'I have it!' she called. 'We are returning.'

Shortly afterwards, they were free of the chamber and standing back in the room with the others.

'It looks exactly the same,' Spike said, as he watched Neeza clip the crystal back onto her necklace. 'Exactly the same as before. And yet …'

Duke gazed at the tiny crystal. 'How on earth could something *that* size grab everything in there and not even show it?'

Jophan slipped an arm about his sister's shoulders.

'We, too, are continually amazed by the crystals,' he said. 'One day, we hope to understand their inter-dimensional capabilities better. Father says we are as yet too young.'

He looked longingly at the crystal, as if he were begging it to give up its secrets.

'I know how you feel,' said Doc. 'It would be so wonderful to know. What I wouldn't give ...'

She stopped. Outside in the corridor, beyond the door through which they'd entered, was a sound. It echoed slightly, and there was another sound. It was a voice raised in alarm. Footsteps sounded faintly in the distance.

'Oh hell,' Duke hissed. 'What do we do now?'

'We've got to get out,' said Terri. 'Someone will be coming in.'

Meatball rushed across to the door. 'I'll peep out. If there's a gap, we can make a run for it.'

Spike followed, tugging on his arm. 'No, that's too dangerous. They'll see us.'

He glanced frantically around the room.

'There is perhaps a way out through the shaft,' Jophan suggested. 'But only Neez and Doc are able to fit.'

'Another *door*! There's another door!'

'What?'

Billy was at the other end of the room, standing before a second doorway. 'It was here all the time,' he said. 'We couldn't have seen it.'

'But how ...?'

The others dashed across to the second doorway. 'Where's it go?'

'Who cares? We can't stay here.'

Wrenching the door open, they rushed through.

As he followed the others through the doorway and into a long corridor, Duke leaned across to grab Spike's arm.

'*That door wasn't there before! We'd have seen it!*'

Spike glanced back at him. 'I know,' he said. 'But what choice have we got?'

Shutting the door carefully behind them, Spike turned to follow the others down the corridor.

It hadn't been there before. That door had not been there, he was sure of that, so had it appeared only for them? After all, it wasn't the first time something like that had happened on one of their missions: something suddenly materialising from out of nowhere when they needed it most. But would the second door still be there when the people outside burst into the room?

Looking back over his shoulder, he gave the wall behind them another quick glance. There was no door. The wall had completely healed over.

He glanced across at Duke. 'What the hell?'

Duke threw up his hands.

They looked up at the sound of Terri's voice. 'You look weird, Meatball, what's up?

'I know this place,' he said. 'I know it, I've seen it before.'

He looked back at them. 'That door, this corridor. I've seen it before, but I've never been here.' He held his head. 'What's going on?'

'You tell me,' Duke said. 'That door thing we escaped through? It's healed over. You know, like yours do, Jo. Spike and I saw it. It healed over and disappeared.'

Terri glanced behind them at a blank wall. 'That's impossible!'

'Not any more it isn't,' Billy said.

Meatball gave a soft cry. 'It's her! The woman … the woman I saw in my vision! I can see her!'

The others looked around them. 'Where?'

Meatball pointed straight ahead. 'There!'

'He's having one of his visions again,' Terri said. 'Where is she, Meatball? Where?'

But Meatball was already striding away, his long legs carrying him in great strides, clearly following something or someone. They didn't bother asking any more questions: they just followed.

As Meatball approached a corner, he stopped. A second corridor ran across the top. Another T-junction: another set of exits both ways. Anxiously, he glanced one way and then the other.

Terri appeared at his side with the others close behind. 'Which way now?'

Billy leaned out to look. The corridors were identical, both long and empty and both stretching off into the distance.

'Which one do we take?'

Duke looked up and down the corridors. 'We can't stand here,' he said. 'This place could be swarming with people soon.'

Meatball stared at the wall. 'It's all right, I can see her again.'

'You sure it's the same woman, Meatball?'

'Yes,' he said, slowly. 'It's definitely the same woman. She's wearing that uniform. She ...'

His eyes softened. 'I can see her face. She's looking at me. She's smiling ... I know her, I'm sure I do, but I've never seen her before.' He turned to them, tears glistening in his eyes. 'How's that possible?'

He stared straight ahead again. 'She's beckoning to us and telling us to follow.'

They followed the corridor as it stretched ahead, curving in a gradual bend around another corner, and came face to face with a gleaming blank wall. A dead end.

'So much for your mystery woman,' Spike snapped, and at once regretted it. They were all stressed and anxious and the visions weren't Meatball's fault. Sometimes he'd been their only hope. 'Sorry Meatball.'

But Meatball scarcely seemed to have heard. He faced the wall ahead, frowning, and obviously completely bewildered himself.

'I don't understand this,' he muttered. 'She said this way. The woman ... she was telling me. She told me it was this way.'

'Well, it obviously *isn't* this way,' Duke interrupted, 'so we'll have to double back. Come on, quick! Meatball! Meatball, come on!'

Meatball stared straight ahead. 'She's back. She's saying it's this way …'

Without waiting for the others, he plunged after the woman and disappeared through the solid wall like a ripple on a pond.

One by one, they followed and the wall swallowed them.

CHAPTER TWENTY

In the filthy surroundings of the timber building that was serving as his temporary home in the past, Gullivan sat on his bed in the dark.

Waking up that morning with the mother of all hangovers, it had taken him almost half an hour to remember what had happened and why he was in the middle of the woods, but now, gradually, piece by irritating piece, it was coming back to him.

The kids. Those revolting, interfering little brats from the village. They'd been here in the past. Here, in his hut and in his way. Again.

The fog in his mind began to clear. Four of them. The spiky haired kid, the girl and two of them aliens. That's all. Four of them.

'And I put them in the stockade!' he yelled at the wall. 'I put them all in the bloody stockade! There's no way they could have got out!'

He took a gulp from a nearby bottle. But they had, hadn't they? They *had* got out. They must have got out, because they were here in his hut, with all their mates when he woke up. With a jolt, he remembered the nightmare he'd had. He'd seen *all* of them: all the kids and the two aliens, just staring at him. He'd sat up in bed and there they were - the ones in the stockade, and the rest of them.

A wave of nausea rose inside him as he remembered the rest. *He'd seen himself.* Vaguely, he remembered screaming and running out of the door. Gullivan shook his head, trying to get the picture out of his mind. How in God's name could he have seen himself?

He stared down at the filthy floor, strewn with bottles. He'd been hallucinating again. That stuff was going to kill him. If he didn't knock it on the head, it was going to kill him.

He kicked out at an empty bottle, sending it spinning across the floor.

Those damned kids. Whenever he saw them, they were trouble.

One thing was obvious. Somehow, those other kids must have followed through the time portal and got the rest of them out, but how?

He thought of the ignorant savage he'd questioned earlier.

Questioned? He snorted. That was a laugh. He could never make these native idiots understand anything. All that fool had done was keep bowing and scraping and pointing at him, as if *he'd* had something to do with letting them out.

He'd felt like punching him, but that would never do. At the moment, he had these peasants right where he wanted them, and he just needed to keep them on side until he had enough plunder to take back with him. Then it was goodbye Roman Britain and he'd be out of here for good.

He took another drink while he thought about other things that didn't make sense.

The badly injured soldier, for one. He'd been at death's door, so how did he make a full recovery?

Gullivan hadn't bothered much at school, but he'd recognised bits of Latin when that soldier had started gibbering about angels. Little one, he'd said, long hair.

His eyes narrowed. Not one of the aliens then.

He threw back his head, laughing. No, it couldn't be them, could it, they were too busy saving the world.

Hang on though … those aliens … what was it that female one had said? A nuclear catastrophe? They were back on Earth to prevent a nuclear catastrophe?

'Yeah, right,' he said. 'Like they're capable of doing that, even assuming there's going to be one.'

His brain whirled. Not that he'd know even if there was, would he, living in the past. Suppose something had happened in the twenty-first century while he was away?

'Oh, for crying out loud,' he shouted. 'Get a grip.'

It was odd, though, now he thought about it. The alien creatures didn't seem the type to be emotional or make up stories, and she'd come out with all that so calmly. He swallowed hard. What if she was telling the truth? What if something *had* happened, and now there was nothing on the other side of the portal, just the aftermath of a nuclear holocaust. That could explain why they were here. A second thought chilled him. What if he couldn't go back? He broke out in a cold sweat. He had to get back. What the hell use would all these baubles be here? If he couldn't get back to cash them in, these damn things might just as well be lumps of plastic.

Picking up a bottle, he threw it against at the wall where it bounced and hit the table, cracking across the base and releasing the amber liquid.

Maybe it was time to go home: time to cut his losses and run. He had quite a big haul of little 'gifts' to cash in: more than enough to buy him everything he wanted in the twenty-first century, including protection from the McKendricks.

Walking across to the time portal, Gullivan leaned down and picked up his shotgun.

Just in case. He now knew Toby McKendrick was in the village. And he wasn't there on holiday.

CHAPTER TWENTY-ONE

The darkness was almost complete, save for the light of a waning moon reflected in the tiny puddles scattered along the edges of the road. A slight breeze, warm, and infused with the scent of damp pavements and brickwork, whispered among the leaves of a nearby tree. It caressed Spike's face, and ruffled his hair.

He stumbled forward into the gloom, almost careering into Meatball as he looked wildly around, trying to catch a glimpse of the woman in uniform.

'She's gone!' He turned to look at them. 'The woman, she was beckoning to me, telling me to follow her.' He shook his head in frustration and disbelief. 'She's gone. How can she be gone? How could she be right in front of me and just disappear? She couldn't have…'

Duke looked about them. 'Where are we?'

They looked warily around, peering into the darkness as their eyes struggled to adjust after the brightness of the research facility.

Buildings rose up in front and to the side, the familiar shapes of houses, windows and doors. Moonlight was mirrored in the cold surface of the taped glass in nearby shop windows.

'It looks kind of familiar,' Doc said. She took several steps forward, trying to get her bearings and recognising some things but not others. 'We're not … we're not *home*, are we?'

Jophan grabbed her sleeve. 'You know this place?'

'Yes, I think so,' Terri said. 'Doc's right, it does look sort of familiar. It looks like the village square. And yet it doesn't.'

'There must be loads of village squares that look like ours,' Duke said.

'You know *why*,' said Meatball, with sudden certainty. 'You know why it looks like it?'

He paused to gaze around him, craning his neck to get a clearer view. 'That little shop on the corner, the building next to it ... and there's the old gatehouse! It's a bank now. It *is* the village square. It is.'

'But not *today*,' Billy breathed. 'Not our time.'

'It's not easy to see in the dark,' said Terri. Leaning backwards, she looked up at the side of the tall dark brickwork next to her, and saw faint shadows of a painted advertisement in the reflected moonlight of the puddle. 'This is barely visible in our time,' she said, 'but I'm sure it's the same one.'

'You know what we've done,' Spike said, stunned. 'We've jumped again.'

'Of *course*.'

Duke stepped off the pavement and wandered across the road and around the corner, the others following close behind. 'This looks familiar, as well,' he said, swinging around to try to get his bearings, 'I know where we are.' He pointed to the shop window directly in front of them. 'This is the Post Office now, isn't it?'

Spike nodded. 'It's the village square, all right. But Bill's right, this isn't our time.' He stared at the windows and something suddenly clicked in his mind. 'We're in the *war*,' he said. 'Look at those windows, they're all taped up! They did that, then, didn't they? Taped them up to stop them smashing in the air raids.'

'The Second World War! Wow! We're in the Second World War, we're doing this at school!'

Doc nodded, furiously.

'My grandad told me all about this,' said Meatball. 'His dad was in the war. And we're really here!'

'We know of this.' Jophan looked about him in wonder. 'It is a truly dramatic part of your history.'

Neeza caught her breath. 'And we are *here* in the middle of it.'

'We might be,' Terri said. 'And if we're not careful, we're going to be seen by somebody and then we'll be right in it.'

'She's right,' said Meatball. 'You couldn't just wander around in them days, not without ID of some sort. And you were supposed to have your gas masks.'

Duke glanced at Jophan and Neeza. 'And how are we going to explain you two?'

'Well, we're not much better off,' Doc said. 'We're hardly dressed right, either. We need some 1940's stuff. Kids didn't dress like this, then. What happens when they see our trainers?'

'So where do we get 1940's stuff?'

'*Here* ...'

Billy was peering in through the shop window. 'Maybe there'll be clothes in this shop. I bet if we look round the back, we can find a way in.'

'But that's stealing,' said Terri. 'What if they catch us?'

'We'll have to make sure they don't,' Duke said. 'Anyway, we haven't got much choice, have we? If we get caught in this lot, we're going to be in trouble.'

'We'll just have to do it.' Spike said. 'Come on, let's have a look round the back.'

They slipped quietly around the side of the shop, keeping close to the wall and feeling their way along the rough brickwork to the next corner, waiting as Duke peered around the edge. 'There's a yard,' he hissed.

At the corner, two rickety wooden gates rose up in front of them.

'We'll have to climb over here, that wall's too high,' said Duke. He turned to Meatball. 'Give us a lift up,' he said. 'I'll look over and see what's there.'

Meatball bent down and made a step with his hands and Duke clambered up and peered over the top of the fence.

'Watch the noise,' Doc hissed. 'We're going to be in big trouble if anyone hears us. There were terrible penalties for looting during the war.'

'Yeah, we know, Doc,' Spike said. 'We all did it at school. But we've got to get some stuff, haven't we?'

'We've got to get some clothes for Jo and Neeza, at least,' Billy said. 'Perhaps a balaclava or something.'

'There's a back door,' Duke hissed, stepping down. 'There's a window as well, but it's far too high up, it'll have to be the door.' He ran a hand across his head. 'Now all we've got to do is figure out how to open it. The gate's ok, I've had a look. It's just a latch.'

Reaching forward, Duke turned the ring on the outside very carefully, eased the gate open, and then gently released it and they stepped inside the yard.

In one corner there was a large metal tank with a tap smelling faintly of paraffin. A tin bath hung from a hook on the wall, casting an eerie outline in the moonlight. A large mangle stood in the shadow.

Lengths of wood and piping had been stacked haphazardly in the opposite corner where empty packing cases stacked on the ground looked ready to topple over. In the farthest corner beyond the door, were two large wooden crates lined with straw. Each held a huge glass bottle.

Picking their way past tightly-bound rolls of chicken wire and corrugated sheets, they tiptoed as quietly as they could past the washing line that swayed slightly in the warm breeze, and over to the back door.

'There's a lock,' said Duke squinting in the darkness. He bent down and peered into the lock, but it was impossible to see.

Jophan stepped forward, put his hands on the door, and closed his eyes. 'You are correct,' he whispered. 'The key protrudes from the lock.' His hands felt along the door, top to bottom. 'There are bolts, also. Here … and here.' Turning to them, his orange eyes shone. 'I can do this, but whether I can move them without sound, I do not know.'

'Give it a try, Jo,' Spike said. 'See how you get on.'

'If it starts to make a noise, we'll have to leave it,' Terri warned. 'See if we can find something else.'

Duke nodded. 'Try it.'

Closing his eyes once more, Jophan leaned against the door. 'It is moving … the key is turning …'

Spike heard a slight *click*! 'Sounds like the lock's free. Have a go at the bolts.'

Head down, Jophan reached up to the top of the door, closed his eyes, and began to concentrate.

Moments later, he stopped and gave a sigh. 'The bolts are stiff and heavy.' He turned to Neeza, who stepped to his side. 'Together.'

Neeza nodded and put her hands to the door. 'They are moving,' she said, 'it is slight, but they are moving.'

The scraping sound was dull but still worryingly loud in the quiet of the yard.

'Stop!' Meatball's voice was also a little too loud. He grabbed Duke's shoulder. 'Stop! *Now!*'

They looked at him.

'What is it?'

'Something's coming.'

'What?'

Even in the darkness, Spike saw the fear on Meatball's face.

'Something's coming!' he snapped in a low growl. 'I'm telling you, something's coming!'

'What sort of thing?'

'I don't know, but we've got to get out of here! There's something coming!'

He threw out his arms in a feeble effort to protect them. 'There's no time!' he cried. '*Get down!*'

CHAPTER TWENTY-TWO

'Get *down!*'

Meatball's startled cry jolted them into action. No need to ask why, no need to question his warning. He knew, he always knew.

Instinctively, they threw themselves onto the hard, concrete floor of the yard and huddled together, heads down, arms stretched around each other's shoulders. A few moments of eerie silence followed and then, in the closeness of the huddle, Spike became aware of a sound: a faint snatch of droning. It grew louder as it approached, the sound dipping intermittently. Something high above them had a faltering engine, and it was getting nearer.

'That sounds like a plane,' Spike breathed. 'That's a *propeller...*'

Jumping to their feet, they stared up in the direction of the sound into a sky littered with wisps of grey cloud. The droning was heavier and clearer now, spluttering and choking, stopping and starting: the last gasps of a dying engine.

And then, out of the gloom, there it was. Dark, solid and heavy, the plane was low and barely a few hundred yards away, gliding noiselessly towards the shop.

'It's coming for us! It's coming for us!' Meatball screamed. 'Get inside!'

Spike lunged for the door handle, yanking it open with such force that it almost flew off its hinges. In a mad scramble, he and the others pushed their way inside and crouched down on the floor, curling into a tight ball.

'Get down!' Duke yelled. 'For God's sake, get down!'

Terri held onto Doc, Neeza and Jophan curled beside her. 'It can't end like this! It can't!'

Trembling, Spike muttered beneath his breath. 'Please God, don't let it hit us! If it hits us, we're dead!'

Gripping Billy, he closed his eyes and waited for the inevitable.

The deafening crash came seconds later as the ailing aircraft ripped across the fabric of the roof, the huge fuselage scoring and sliding across timber and tiles and almost shearing the top off the building before continuing through the night sky.

The whole building quaked with shock. It creaked, shuddered and groaned, the floor above them booming with the sounds of falling timber and bricks. Board and plaster rained down on them like a lumpy snowstorm. Curled tightly together, they prayed the whole ceiling wouldn't give way and collapse on top of them.

When finally the house stopped moaning, Spike cautiously lifted his head. It was difficult to see: the air was thick with swirling dust. At the slightest movement, plaster tumbled into their hair and faces.

'I can't *see* ...'

He looked across at Terri. She was gasping, her eyes streaming.

'Keep your eyes closed for a bit.' Meatball bent over with the effort, coughing and choking. 'Till it settles.'

Duke nodded, sending a cloud of dust over Billy. 'Sorry, mate ...'

In sudden alarm, Spike swung around to check Jophan and Neeza. 'Jo! Neeza! Are you ok?'

Tucked protectively beside Neeza, Jo lifted his head. 'We are well.' He stopped to cover his mouth. 'But this dust ...'

'Pull your jumper up over your mouth!' Doc said. 'It helps.'

Duke got stiffly to his feet and stared around. 'Everyone all right?'

A mingled chorus of answers reached him through the haze.

Terri pulled herself up onto a nearby table. 'My legs won't stop shaking. What happened? A bomb or something?'

Brushing the muck from his clothes, Meatball straightened up, pulled a torch from his pocket, and flicked it on. 'We wouldn't be here to ask, if it had been a bomb.'

Through the hazy beam, they stared around at the devastation. Shattered plaster strewn about the floor, lumps of timber hanging from the ceiling, furniture almost obscured beneath a layer of dust.

'The plane must've hit us,' Doc said. 'There's no way it could've have missed. Not that low, it must've hit the roof. Taken half of it off probably.'

'Thank God this old place is still standing,' Duke said. 'We could have been killed.'

'And the *noise*,' Doc whispered. 'My ears are still ringing. What must it have been like in a bombing raid?'

'Terrifying,' Spike said, hoarsely. He glanced up at the ceiling where odd lumps of plaster were still detaching themselves to fall to the ground. Wisps of dust trickled slowly from one or two cracks. 'We're lucky it never caved right in,' he said. 'But it doesn't look very safe, that lot could come down at any moment. We'd better get out while we can.'

Stumbling over the rubble, they helped each other towards the door which was now half open. Through the gap, the faint creamy-grey dust was being sucked outside to clear rapidly in the breeze. They clustered around the opening, leaning toward the flow of fresh air, gasping in breaths.

'*Wait guys, hang on!*'

'What?'

Terri was gazing upwards, listening. 'I can hear something! Spike, I can hear something! Something upstairs.'

Duke and Jophan stepped back over the piles of debris. 'It's probably things creaking or splitting or something.'

Jophan glanced upwards. 'It may be that the ceiling is on the point of collapse. It is not safe to remain.'

'No … no, Terri is right. I, too, can hear something,' Neeza said. 'A faint voice …'

Meatball frowned up at the ceiling. 'Perhaps we should take a look.'

Billy suddenly darted toward the door of the room and pulled it open. Dust showered down on him. 'I heard something, too!'

'Bill! *Wait!*'

Spike lunged after him, grabbing Billy's coat as he jumped onto the staircase. 'Wait, for goodness sake! We don't know that this staircase is safe. Hang on!'

A faint cry drifted down to them from upstairs.

Pushing past them, Terri listened. 'Told you! Someone's calling.'

They waited quietly, listening for any sound or movement, but it had stopped.

Duke cupped his hands and yelled. '*Hello?*'

Again, a faint cry.

'I heard it that time!'

Jophan surged forward. 'There is a response, we must help!'

'Take it slow! Test each step.'

Treading gently, one step at a time, Spike and Meatball made their way slowly up the staircase and onto the landing, followed by the others.

'Hello?' Duke called. 'Where are you?'

'*Here*! We're in *here*! Help us!'

The voice was louder now: desperate, pleading, calling for help.

'We're coming!' yelled Terri.

Duke grasped the handle and then threw all his weight against it, but it wouldn't budge. Squeezing in beside him, Meatball and Jophan braced their feet against the floor and pushed as hard as they could.

'It must be locked.'

'More likely blocked with rubble,' said Spike, pushing through. 'Here, let me have a go.'

He tried pushing and then kicking the door, bringing clouds of debris down onto their heads.

'Watch it! You'll have us all buried!'

'I've got to be able to do it,' he muttered. 'I've got to.'

'Wait!' The others leaned against the door beside him. 'Together. One ... two ...'

With one enormous heave, they pushed on the door and it edged gradually open, scraping and scoring across the wooden floor until Spike staggered into the room.

'Where are you?'

'*Here...*' The weak voice came from somewhere in the far corner.

Squinting in the suffocating dust, Spike peered through the gloom. In the centre of the room, the air was slowly clearing, whipped around by a strong breeze.

Above them, a large part of the roof was now a gaping hole ripped away by the collision. Huge wooden struts swayed loosely in the breeze. The corner of the room was almost completely obscured by rubble and other large pieces of timber, but in the distance he could just make out the frame of a bed.

'*Help us ...*'

The voice grew fainter.

'We're coming,' Terri called. 'Don't worry, we're coming.'

Carefully, they clambered over piles of shifting rubble, picking their way over sharp masonry and bricks, huge posts and dangerous shards of timber, studded with protruding nails that scraped their legs and hands.

'We're coming.' Billy's feet slipped and slid across the floor. 'We're coming to help y...'

He started to cough again as the dust and splinters robbed him of his voice.

'Keep your jumpers up over your mouths,' Duke called.

Beside him, Spike leaned across, seized the shattered remains of a huge wooden lintel and pulled with all his strength.

'Look out!' Duke yelled, as the rubble beneath started to shift. 'The rest of it's coming down with it!'

Meatball shone the torch into the corner. Almost hidden by bricks and timber, the top of a bed was the only part clearly visible. Passing the torch to Terri, he bent down to clear a jagged lump of stone.

Duke and Jophan grabbed it, rolled it away, and took each end of the large post beneath.

'We need more light!' Duke hissed.

Jophan whirled around. 'Neez! The crystal!'

'Of course! I wonder?' She closed her eyes. On the golden chain around her neck, the tiny crystal started to glow.

Doc looked up from where she and Terri were clearing rubble from their path. 'Watch the light, Neez! Remember it's wartime!'

'I shall be careful.' From the base of the crystal, she directed the beam to splay out across the bed and floor.

As they stumbled nearer, Spike saw the top half of a man twisted to one side as if to protect someone near him. Slowly, he turned his head to look at them. His face was bleeding.

'My wife,' he croaked, over a parched throat. 'My wife … please help her …'

His eyes closed and he sank back onto the pillow.

Reaching across, Terri took his hand in hers. 'Don't worry,' she said. 'We'll get you out.'

Duke glanced across at the bed. Hefty wooden posts had fallen across the covers and on top of these lay all that remained of the chimneystack: mounds of broken bricks and mortar.

Climbing around the edge of the bed, the boys worked together to lift heavy blocks of crumbling brick and heave them to one side and then to pass them to Billy and the girls. By the light of the crystal, they worked swiftly and carefully, moving enough of the bricks to free the cumbersome timber posts lying across the man and his wife.

Doc had squeezed through to the other side of the bed and was now looking down at the man's wife, who lay still and lifeless. 'Hurry guys, I think she's badly hurt! Her breathing sounds bad!'

Carefully, she reached down to brush dust and plaster from the woman's face and shoulders. The woman showed no response.

Doc and Terri exchanged anxious looks.

At the end of the bed, Spike lifted the last and heaviest of the timber beams and pushed it onto the floor.

Doc sat on the bed and closed her eyes. 'I see it,' she said. 'The light. It's filling my mind.'

Once again, she put her hands to her face and then slowly lowered them down to the woman's chest.

Gradually, the woman's laboured breathing eased into a quiet, steady rhythm.

Doc moved to the other side of the bed, where she used her healing powers once more and the man breathed easy.

Exhausted, she slumped forward, her head in her hands. Terri hugged her. 'Well done, Doc.'

'I hope so ... I think they're going to be ok.'

'You were fantastic, Doc ... hello, where's the light gone?'

'The light's gone out ...'

The crystal had switched off, plunging them once more into semi-darkness.

'Neez! The crystal!

'I cannot! It will not!'

'And I think I know why,' hissed Meatball, listening.

'There's people coming. Let's get out! Bill, the torch!'

Flicking on the torch, Billy shone the beam downwards to light their way as they stumbled across the room, heading for the door.

'*Wait* ...!'

They stopped suddenly and looked around. The man was sitting up, gazing at them and holding out a hand. Beside him, his wife opened her eyes and leaned up on one elbow. 'Wait! Please, kids, whoever you are. We want to thank you.' Terri smiled. 'We have to leave,' she said, gently. 'I'm sorry, we have to go now. You'll be ok, someone's coming.'

'But … but wait … who are you?'

The man jerked as, in the reflected light of the torch, his eyes fell on the faces of Jophan and Neeza. For a moment or two, his mouth moved soundlessly. Then he spoke.

'*What* are you …?'

CHAPTER TWENTY-THREE

By the time they stopped to catch their breath, they'd been running in fits and starts for almost ten minutes.

Bursting through the back door, they dashed across the yard and out into a deserted lane and then sprinted down a narrow passageway, the distant shouts of rescuers arriving at the shop floating faintly after them on the breeze.

Duke peered carefully around the corner at the end of the passageway, and then they stepped into the stark emptiness of a familiar road and instinctively followed it along its entire length until it turned off into the park. Flopping down onto the ground, they rested for a moment to catch their breath and think about their next move.

The park was larger than he remembered, with no barriers or fencing, just sprawling fields and the reassuring cover of towering trees.

'The park seems much bigger,' said Billy. 'Different somehow. It doesn't look the same.'

Spike twisted slowly around, trying to get his bearings. 'I think I've got it,' he said, carefully. 'Over there, in the distance, I think that's Parsons Field, where the new housing estate is now. There's the farm, look. That went years ago.'

Duke looked back at the entrance to the park and then swung back to stare out across the open fields. 'You're right. That is Parsons Field.' He leaned further around. 'Which means over *there* must be the old school fields. And beyond that ...'

'Hawketts Wood!' Billy gave a sharp cry of recognition. 'Hawketts Wood is that big black area over there. You can see the outline of the trees.'

'Which means Gullivan's land isn't far away either,' Duke said.

'But it wasn't Gullivan's land in the war, was it?'

'No.'

'I remember Gran saying someone called Forester used to live there years ago.' Spike frowned, trying to remember. 'He had a son who was in the war, I think.'

'Well, that doesn't help us, does it?' Doc snapped, impatiently. 'What do we do now?'

'Father warned this may happen,' said Neeza. 'He said we may have to find our way back to our own time.'

'Yeah, great,' Terri said. 'But *how*?'

'What about Solomon?' said Billy. 'Solomon will help us. If the wood is over that way, then Solomon will be there somewhere. Won't he?'

They were silent for a moment, remembering the great oak tree. '*Solomon*,' Spike whispered, 'I don't know.'

Billy opened his hands. 'He's got to *be* there, he can't be anywhere else, can he? Of course, he'll be about eighty years younger.'

Meatball shook his head. 'He won't be burnt out in*side* either.'

'But Solomon isn't the tree,' Spike said. 'Solomon's the time portal. He only opens in the tree when he wants to, remember?'

He became aware of Jophan and Neeza staring at him. 'This Solomon you speak of. He can help us?'

'No,' he admitted. 'Well, not like that. He's not a person.' He scratched his head. 'Surely, there must be another way.'

'There is, of course, the old railway station,' Jophan said, calmly. 'That has a time portal, does it not? Assuming we can locate it.'

'Oh, my goodness!' Terri cried. 'Of course! Brilliant, Jo! The *station!* Why didn't we think of that?'

Meatball looked thoughtful. 'Wait a minute, though. That means we'll have to go back through the village.'

'Oh, hell …'

Leaning against a fence post, Doc took a deep breath and straightened up. 'You know, you lot seem to have forgotten something.'

'Have we?'

She looked at them for a moment, before she answered. 'The *plane*.'

'What plane?' Duke asked.

'The plane that just took the roof off! The plane that nearly killed us! What happened to it?'

'Well, it must've kept going, mustn't it? Unless it's crashed somewhere.'

'But what about the pilot, Duke? It must've had a pilot.'

Meatball hung his head. 'If it crashed … well, surely, he must've …'

'He could've bailed out,' said Billy. 'If he knew it was going to crash, he could've bailed out.'

'He could be lying somewhere, injured.'

Doc nodded. 'He could be, Terri. That's the thing. And it occurred to me that maybe we have to deal with that first, before anything else becomes clear.'

They looked at each other, quietly mulling over what Doc had said. Maybe she was right, maybe that *was* part of their mission.

'And if you think about it,' Billy said. 'It can't be coincidence that we came out into the war, just as that couple needed help. I mean, it can't be, can it? Surely, that's got to be meant. I know about your vision, Meatball, about the lady in the uniform 'n' all that, but she could've led us anywhere. Why here?'

'It's a point,' said Duke. 'We must've been meant to help that couple in the shop, and what if Doc's right?' He threw up his hands. 'What if we are supposed to look for the pilot?'

'But where do we start? He could be anywhere. If he bailed out, he could be miles away. Without some sort of clue, we haven't got a chance.'

Terri looked down at the crystal. 'Neez, I don't suppose?'

Neeza shook her head. 'There is nothing.' Slowly, she raised her eyes to look at them. 'It is a possibility, I think, that the poor man may not have survived.'

Spike closed his eyes. 'What else can we do?' He shrugged apologetically. 'I know this sounds awful, but there's us as well. This is wartime, don't forget. If we get caught, we'll never get home.'

'They're bound to be looking for us,' said Meatball. He glanced apprehensively back at the entrance to the Park. 'Those people back there are bound to have told them about us. I've got a feeling that whatever we're doing, we'd better get a move on.'

'Guess you're right.' Duke sighed. 'Our only hope is to make for the station and see what happens.'

They set off around the edge of the field, tucking in behind trees wherever possible and moving stealthily across the open field, where there was no other option. Hawketts Wood was somewhere up ahead, and they kept it in sight as a bearing, but for ages, it didn't seem to be getting any closer: just a black shape outlined against the night sky.

Weak with tiredness, they travelled on across the park until eventually the grass gave way to stout trunks and roots and the gloom of dense woodland.

Amid the sounds of the night, Spike became aware of the faint trickling of water. 'The river!'

Deeper in the wood, the gentle sounds of the river became clearer. 'It has to be round here somewhere. It runs right through the wood.'

He paused by the trunk of a large tree and looked down onto a rippled surface as moonlight filtered through the trees. 'Here it is! If we follow this, we should come out at the top of Gullivan's field.'

They walked on, stepping over mounds and tree roots and following the natural path, pushing through, into a small clearing

The stillness was broken by a loud *crunch*.

Duke swung around. 'What's that?'

'Think I've trodden on something,' said Billy.

'Probably just a branch.' Meatball stepped across and shone the torch.

Billy looked down. Something lay on the ground, glinting in the torchlight. Gingerly, he bent down to pick it up.

'What have you got, Bill?'

Billy held the thing up to the light for them all to see. It was a pair of goggles with a badly smashed lens. 'I trod on them.'

Leaning forward, Duke took the goggles in his hand. 'They're pilot goggles,' he said. 'Flying goggles. I've seen them before, at that air show we went to last summer. There was a Spitfire there, and ...'

'The pilot!' cried Jophan. 'These then, may belong to the pilot we seek?'

'*Surely* ...'

'They've got to. They've got to be his. It's too much of a coincidence.'

'You're right, Duke, these are definitely flying goggles,' Spike said, studying them. 'And if they do belong to the pilot, he can't be too far away.'

'Unless he's already gone,' Doc said. 'He might already have gone. Maybe he parachuted down and he's gone back to the village or something.'

'Or *may*be he's crashed somewhere and he's lying injured. How are we supposed to know?'

Billy pointed upwards, directly above their heads. 'Here, guys ... what's that there? Is that him?'

Terri peered up into the gloom and gave a sudden gasp. Her arm shot up, her hand pointing into the trees. 'I can see him! There he *is*!'

CHAPTER TWENTY-FOUR

Crowded around the base of the tree, they peered upwards. Several feet above, a figure was hanging by his parachute, tangled among the stout branches.

Duke gazed up at the figure, trying to see if he was moving, but it was just a still shape in the darkness.

'We've got to get him down, but how?'

'His parachute looks in a right mess,' said Meatball. 'It's all caught up. We'll have to climb up there and cut him out.'

Billy flicked on the torch.

'No, Bill, switch it off,' Spike said. 'Don't shine it upwards whatever you do. This is war-time. We'll just have to get up there as best we can. Have you still got that penknife on you?'

Billy pulled the penknife from his pocket and passed it to Spike, who gently stroked the edge of the blade with his thumb.

'Dunno if it'll be sharp enough, but we can give it a go.'

'We shall do it,' Jophan interrupted, holding out his hand for the knife. 'Climbing is a skill natural to our people.'

'But...'

'We shall do it,' said Neeza. Turning, she ran at the tree and in one bound leaped from the ground and grasped the tree trunk.

Behind her, Jophan bounded into the tree and almost ran up it with ease, clambering over trunk and branches like a squirrel and slowly disappearing into the darkness.

'They weren't kidding, were they?'

Spike watched them in astonishment. 'They're like Spiderman.'

'That's quite high up,' said Terri, nervously, straining to see through the branches. 'I hope they're going to be all right.'

Meatball leaned against the trunk, peering upwards. 'It's not too bad, I can still see them.' He called out to them, softly. 'How's it going, Jo?'

'All is well,' came the reply. 'We are moving along the branches.'

'For goodness sake, be careful!' Duke called.

'I have located the cords.' Jophan's voice drifted down between the leaves above. 'They are very tangled.'

'How is he? Is he ok? Can you see?'

'It is difficult to be sure.' Neeza's voice came from slightly lower down the tree. 'He is, I think, still breathing. But there is no movement.'

'We need to get him down as quick as we can,' Doc said. 'It sounds as though I need to help him.'

'Stay where you are, Jo, we're coming up!' Duke turned to the others. 'Spike, you stay down here, we're going to need your strength at the bottom. Meatball, you, and me will climb up and see if we can lower him down. We should be able to do it between us.'

Spike nodded.

Duke looked about him. 'We could do with something *else* … something to use as a safety net …'

'We'll wrap the cords around a branch,' said Meatball. 'Lower him down slow. We'll manage somehow.'

'I'll take the weight,' said Spike. 'Piece of cake.'

Terri looked at him. 'This is a full-grown man.'

Duke and Meatball began to climb.

Spike shrugged. 'Yanked a tree out, didn't I? There must be a reason I've got this strength. Anyway, I've got Bill and you two.'

'Yep,' she said, breezily. 'Guess you're just lucky.'

Even in the darkness, Terri could see him grin.

Leaning against the trunk, Spike listened. 'How's it going?'

'We are endeavouring to wrap the cords around a heavy branch,' Jophan answered. 'They are difficult to unravel.'
'Ok,' he called. 'Let me know when you're ready.'
Several minutes passed. At the base of the tree, they watched and listened to the others moving among the branches, as broken twigs, leaves and fragments of bark fell through the air at intervals to land on the ground beside them.
Spike stared up the tree. 'What's happening?'
'I think we've got it,' said Meatball.
'Get ready!' Duke called. 'We going to try lowering him down. You there, Spike?'
'Yeah, start bringing him down!'
Staring upwards into the gloom, they waited breathlessly, and then gradually, out of the tree, two leather boots swayed into view.
'Here he comes!' Spike rushed across to take hold of the man's body. 'Give us a hand!'
'We've got him!'
Little by little, the pilot descended out of the tree. Supporting his legs, Terri and Doc eased them steadily forward as Spike took the full weight of the body, Billy supporting the man's shoulders and head.
Gently, he was lowered to the ground, cushioning him as best they could, slowly, slowly, and down onto the soft earth.
Duke yelled from up in the tree. 'You got him ok?'
'Yes, we've got him!'
Suddenly, the small space was full of sound as the others clambered out of the tree. One by one, they dropped to the ground.
Crouching down, Spike carefully loosened the helmet and clothing.
Doc bent over the still figure on the ground, Neeza beside her. A soft purple glow suddenly crept from the base of the crystal.
'He's breathing,' Doc said. 'But only *just*.'

Spike watched as Doc closed her eyes, and waited for the warm glow to overwhelm her as it seeped through and down into the broken body on the ground.

For several long minutes, the others waited. Doc seemed almost trance-like, her head bowed, her breathing shallow.

'Doc? You ok?'

Duke turned to the others. 'Is she ok? She doesn't …'

At that moment, Doc drew in a long gasp and fell back on her heels. 'I've done all I can,' she said.

The pilot's eyes remained closed but his breathing was quiet and regular.

Terri appeared beside Doc and the body. In her hand, she held her scarf, sopping wet from a dip in the river. Gently, she wetted the man's lips and wiped his face.

For a long moment, the pilot lay still, bathed in the gentle purple light as they gazed down at him.

'He really needs to be covered,' Doc whispered. 'It's a warm night, but he's in shock.'

'He can have my coat,' said Spike. He slipped it from around his waist and ripped out the labels as best he could.

'What if someone finds it?'

'Then they do. We'll just have to hope no one looks too closely at it. We can't leave him to get cold, can we?'

He bent down and draped his coat across the motionless body.

Terri squeezed Spike's arm. 'No, we can't. We can share stuff. It'll be cold when we get home.'

Billy bent down to add his scarf.

'If we ever want to *see* home, we need to get a move on,' Duke said. 'Will he be ok, Doc?'

'I wish he would move,' said Jophan, kneeling down beside him. 'I would feel easier leaving him if there was a response.'

As he spoke, the pilot's eyes twitched and then slowly opened. Immediately, they threw themselves back out of sight.

On his knees beside him, Jophan started and then struggled to his feet, fumbling with his hood and trying to replace it before the pilot caught a glimpse of his face.

Duke grabbed Meatball's arm. 'Time to go,' he whispered. 'Let's get out of here. *Now.*'

With a last glance across at the pilot, they turned and set off through the trees.

'I suppose … you're sure he was ok?' asked Terri. 'We didn't leave him too soon, did we?'

'No. He should be fine,' said Doc. 'He was completely healed, but it'll take him a while to come round.'

'Long enough for us to get well away and home, hopefully,' said Meatball.

In the woods under the cover of the trees, it seemed safer, but it slowed them down.

Billy tried to hide a yawn. 'If we ever *get* home,' he said. 'We don't even know how to get back home yet.'

Spike sighed. 'I think Jo's right,' he said. 'It's got to be the station. It's the only place we know there's a time portal.'

'Yeah, and what if that same time portal takes us back to Gullivan?' asked Terri. 'What if we end up in that awful place again, with him?'

'We won't,' he said.

'Says you. You don't know that.'

'Don't have a go at me, Terri, it's not my fault.'

Terri sat down on a nearby tree stump. 'Sorry, Spike. I'm shattered.'

He yawned. 'Yeah, I know. Me 'n' all.'

Meatball rubbed his eyes. 'We're all shattered.'

'I am.' Doc whispered softly, as much to herself as anyone else. 'I am so tired. It's great, this healing thing, but I'm shattered. I'd give anything to be at home now in my nice warm bed.'

'We should find somewhere to rest,' said Neeza. She looked across at Doc. 'Doc needs to rest.'

Terri glanced at Doc. 'Sorry Doc, we didn't think.'

Duke nodded. 'That settles it. But where?'

'Hang on a minute.' Meatball pointed over into the distance. 'Spike, you mentioned something about the farm ... the one that's gone now, you said?

'Parsons Farm?'

'Yeah, that's the one. And it must still be there now, on the other side of this wood. And where's there a farm, there's a *barn,* and there'll probably be a hay loft.' He looked around at the others. 'What d'you reckon?'

'Sounds good to me,' said Duke. 'Let's make for the farm.'

Doc leaned against a tree. Her legs were trembling. 'I don't think I can walk any more,' she said. 'I'm exhausted. You lot go on.'

Meatball walked across and bent down. 'Yeah, right,' he said. 'On you get, Doc, I'll give you a piggyback.'

'You can't do that, Meatball.'

'Course I can. You only weigh about as much as a flea. If I go face first in the muck at the farm, Duke can take over.'

'Be like Brett Tyler,' said Billy.

In spite of their tiredness, everyone laughed at the thought of Brett Tyler face down in the muck, and they were still chuckling as they finally left the woodland and climbed over the style into the farmer's field.

Now, if they could just locate the hay barn and get some sleep.

CHAPTER TWENTY-FIVE

In the chill of the cowshed, Gullivan leaned over a large trunk, studying a chunky gold necklace by the light of a hissing gas lantern. Studded with precious stones, the necklace shimmered softly in the light.

Despite makeshift repairs to the timber walls, the bitter easterly wind had found every crack and was constantly whipping around his neck, sending shivers down his spine. He tucked a woollen scarf tightly into his jacket, reached into the trunk and retrieved the rest of the collection of artefacts he'd acquired, courtesy of those ignorant fools back in Roman Britain.

He nodded to himself as he dropped the treasures into a bag. With any luck, these little beauties would take care of everything. Especially now he'd found a buyer.

Bringing all this stuff back was one thing, finding someone to buy it was another but he couldn't just put it on the internet. It was all a question of who to trust. He certainly couldn't go back to that scumbag Thorpe, not after last time. He wouldn't forget Thorpe had betrayed him to the McKendricks.

Gullivan dropped the bag into a case and snapped the catches shut.

Thank God for collectors with pots of money and no conscience, he thought. Tomorrow morning, the guy had said. Tomorrow morning, and the money would be his. More than enough to get away from this hellhole, and make a new life.

And he'd never have to go back to Roman Britain again.

Picking up the heavy case, he walked out of the cowshed, crossed the yard through the swirling snow, and stepped into the relative warmth of the kitchen.

The comforting glow of the gas lantern cheered him a little. All in all, it had been a pretty good day.

He walked across to light the primus stove. Filling the kettle, he watched the shivering orange flames lick up the sides.

Just what he needed. A strong cup of black coffee with a slug or two of rum.

He glanced casually out through the window. The snow was billowing around in thick clouds. He could have done without this bad weather. Hopefully, the roads would still be passable tomorrow. The minute he got his hands on that money, he was off.

He thought a bit about the next day as the kettle boiled. Maybe he ought to smarten up a bit. The buyer he'd contacted obviously had pots of money.

He glanced at his face in the chipped shaving mirror that stood on the windowsill and ran a hand over his chin. Maybe a wash and a shave wouldn't be a bad idea: he didn't want the guy to think he was some sort of disreputable low-life.

The steam from the kettle clouded the image for a moment. As it cleared, Gullivan saw something else in the reflection over by the doorway. The one thing he had dreaded seeing.

It was the unmistakeable outline of Toby McKendrick slowly raising his arm and in his hand, glistening in the light, Gullivan saw the unmistakeable outline of a gun.

He didn't have time to think. Seizing the hot kettle by the handle, Gullivan gave it one almighty swing, hurled it through the air in Toby's direction, and leaped for the door.

In that same second, Toby fired.

The bullet sliced into Gullivan's shoulder just as the full weight of the kettle struck Toby on the side of his head, knocking him from his feet.

Gasping with the searing pain, Gullivan collapsed against the doorframe for a moment and then forcing himself onwards, he staggered out of the door and into the blinding snowstorm.

CHAPTER TWENTY-SIX

The following morning, Duke jerked upright from a mass of hay, and listened.

Beside him, Meatball stirred. 'What's that noise?'

Spike scrambled out of his warm hay bed, ran across to the wall of the barn and peered through the cracks. 'It's just the farmer.'

'What's he doing?'

Pulling a warm hoodie tightly around him, Spike continued to watch as the farmer walked to another building and opened the doors. Moments later, a diesel engine burst into life. 'He's getting the tractor out.'

'He might want to come in here,' said Meatball, watching as the tractor pulled alongside the barn. 'For tools or something.'

As they watched from the hayloft above, the doors swung open and a trailer slowly backed in.

'What if he comes up here?' Duke watched anxiously as the farmer leaped down from the tractor. 'Hopefully he won't.'

Spike glanced behind him into the corner. It was stacked high with hay bales. 'Let's get over in the far corner behind those.'

They crawled hurriedly behind the bales, pulling them over and around themselves and peered down through the floorboards, watching anxiously as the farmer loaded up the trailer.

At that moment, another figure appeared at the door of the barn. It was a small woman in a loose cardigan and a floral overall covering her slim body. Her long brown hair fell in

161

curls, clipped up at the sides and topped with a headscarf. In her hand, she had a tin box.

'You'd forget your 'ead if it wasn't screwed on,' she said.

The farmer glanced down at her and smiled.

'Hang on, Flo, I'll switch her off.'

The engine died.

'Your lunch, Jed,' she said, pushing the box toward him. 'You're going to need it today.'

'Thanks, love.'

He leaned across to kiss her cheek and slipped the box onto the seat of the tractor. Then he climbed up beside it and restarted the engine. The tractor roared into life. Thick, black, sooty smoke belched from the exhaust funnel and he pulled slowly away out into the yard, pausing only to leap down and close the huge barn doors before he chugged away up the lane.

Clambering over the bales of hay, Meatball peered out through the side of the barn. 'Gone,' he said.

'Now's our chance,' said Duke. 'We'll go out and along the side of the barn and make our way across the fields to the village. Once we're there, we should be able to find the old station, no problem. Any of that water left?'

'Yeah.' Billy held up a stone jug. 'There's some left in the bottom, but it's full of insects and bits of straw.'

Duke pulled a face. 'Great. What I wouldn't give for a can right now.'

'I'd rather have a bit of chocolate,' said Billy. 'Maybe we could have got some in that kitchen last night.'

'We could hardly hang about looking for chocolate,' Doc said. 'We took enough of a risk going in there at all. Anyway, they probably haven't got any chocolate. This is wartime, remember? You couldn't get sugar, it was on ration.'

'Americans had it,' Spike said, longingly, remembering his history lesson. 'They had loads of it.'

'Can we pack up talking about food?' asked Terri. 'I'm starving. All we've had is that bit of rotten old bread and cheese we found.'

'That was on ration as well,' said Doc.

'Oh, shut up, Doc,' Terri snapped. 'I'm starving.'

'Our first priority is to make for the station,' said Jophan. 'Is it possible there would be any food there?'

'Yeah! I remember Gran saying they had machines on stations for chocolate and stuff!'

Doc pulled a face. 'Chocolate's *rationed*. You'd need the old money anyway. You've got a load of that on you, have you?'

Spike's smile faded. 'Oh.'

'Never mind about grub,' said Meatball. 'We've still got to get out of here without being seen.'

'That, I think, is not our immediate problem,' Neeza said suddenly, peering through another tiny gap in the side of the barn. 'Someone is approaching in the distance.'

Jophan took a look. 'Who is it? The farmer?'

'No, it is more than one person. And a figure of authority, I think.'

Meatball squeezed in beside her and then turned to look at the others. 'That's all we need. It's the police!'

'*The police* ...'

'Well, a policeman, anyway. And a few other people with him.'

'The police? Here, you don't think ...'

Terri held a hand to her mouth. 'You don't think maybe they've found out. About us, I mean. You don't think those people in the shop ... or the pilot ... maybe they told them about us. They might have done.'

'It wouldn't matter if they did, would it? A few kids who helped them out?'

'Wouldn't be just a few kids though, would it, Bill? A kid that healed them? Two others that look like Jo and Neez?'

'And even if they didn't notice our clothes, the police soon will,' Terri said.

163

'It is imperative we are not discovered,' Jophan said.

'Don't worry, Jo,' Spike said. 'We'll think of something.'

'Like what?' said Doc. 'Suppose they knock at the door and speak to the farmer's wife. She might've noticed that food's missing.'

'Well, we'd better think of something fast,' Meatball said.

'They're turning in the end of the track.'

'I've got an idea,' Billy said, smiling.

They turned. 'Well, let's have it then, Bill, quick!'

Billy looked at Duke. 'You can pretend to be the farmer, Duke. You know, change into him and go down and talk to them. If you go out to meet them, they probably won't knock.'

Duke closed his eyes in despair.

Meatball chewed his lip. 'Bet you're real glad that's your special skill, aren't you?'

'It's not funny!' Duke snapped.

'No, sorry mate, I know it's not, but it might be our only chance.'

'It's going to take some guts,' said Spike. 'So it's up to you. Maybe …'

'No! No, I'll do it.' Duke took a deep breath. 'It's our best chance. We know the farmer's gone off to the fields. Maybe I can send them off in the wrong direction or something.'

'Good thinking,' Doc said.

Duke rubbed his chin with his hand. 'Trouble is, I only saw the farmer for a few minutes. What if I don't get it quite right?'

The others gazed thoughtfully at one another. 'It is risky,' Spike said, quietly. 'And dangerous. What if they notice something? What if his wife comes out again?'

'Then you'll have to kiss her,' Terri said. 'Stop her saying anything.'

Duke glared at her. 'You trying to make me puke, or what?'

'They're halfway up the drive!' said Billy, keeping watch through the gap. 'Now would be a good time if you're going to do it.'

Meatball shook his head, vaguely. 'I don't know what to say, Duke, it's got to be your decision.'

Duke closed his eyes for a moment. 'Yeah,' he said. 'I know you're right. If it was one of you who could do it, I'd be saying it was a good idea. But why me? Why did I have to be the one who could do this stupid thing? And what if I can't do it, I only saw him for a few minutes.' His shoulders drooped. 'I'll give it a go.'

They watched, fascinated, as he changed shape completely and became the farmer.

'It's the voice as well, though,' he said. 'How does this sound?'

'Not *bad*,' said Meatball. 'Being honest, I can't remember. Should be ok. Keep it simple, though, or you might mention something that sounds suspicious.'

'We could take our chances,' said Terri. 'Maybe they won't search the barn.'

Duke shook his head. 'Course they will. There's no option, I'll have to do it.'

Walking across to the ladder, he slid down to the floor and then with a last glance back at them, he took a deep breath and stepped out through the barn doors.

'I hope he's ok,' Terri said, anxiously. 'What if they spot something?'

'He *looks* just like him,' Spike said. 'And that's the main thing. They've got no reason to suppose it isn't him, have they?'

'People usually believe what they see with their own eyes,' Doc said. 'God, my heart's pounding, I can't think what Duke's is doing.'

Through the gap, they watched Duke amble away down the lane.

'Perhaps he'll say he's got a bad throat or something?'

Terri's voice died away. As they crouched down beside the gap, Spike watched and prayed.

Halfway down the lane, Duke was trying his best to plod casually on broad, muscled legs, thinking as fast as his beleaguered brain would allow. What if he'd got the look a bit wrong? What if they noticed something? What if he let something slip? What if he mentioned something they'd never heard of before?

Don't say too much, he told himself, say only what you have to.

He looked down the lane to where a group of people were trudging toward him. People from the village, he supposed, with the local police sergeant in front.

They were getting close now, he must stay calm and focused.

'Morning, Jed.' The sergeant stepped towards him.

It was then Duke realised the worst. These people knew the farmer well and he didn't have a clue who they were. Maybe he could get by without mentioning any names. Oh lord, he had to.

'Morning,' he said.

There was a moment's silence. The voice, Duke thought in a panic. I've got the voice wrong.

A short, square man in the crowd suddenly addressed him. 'You got this throat thing 'n' all then, Jed?'

Duke nodded and put a hand to his throat.

To his relief, the police sergeant continued. 'You seen a group of kids about here anywhere? We've been out looking for them since first light.'

Duke thought for a moment, then said, 'Kids?'

'Yeah, six or seven of them, so we reckon. Couple of them are a bit weird looking.'

Duke shook his head. 'No. Not seen 'em round here. What they done, then?

'We just want to talk to them,' the sergeant, said, firmly.

To Duke's horror, another man then said, 'They could be hiding out in that barn of yours.'

Duke's heart thudded. 'Shouldn't think so,' he said. 'I was in there this morning. You can look if you like.'

'I think Jed would know if they were in there, Tom,' the sergeant said, dismissively. He turned to Duke. 'Sorry to bother you, Jed. Let me know if you see them.'

'Will do, Sergeant,' said Duke.

The sergeant gave him a quizzical look. 'We'll be searching in them woods,' he said, slowly. His eyes looked searchingly into Duke's, and then he pointed over in the direction of Hawketts Wood. 'Just over there. If you see anything.'

Duke nodded.

The search party moved away and tramped off across the fields towards the wood.

Behind them, Duke shook with relief. Had he convinced them?

He saw the sergeant give a glance back in his direction, then walk on. No, he wasn't at all sure that he had. They had to leave the barn quickly and move on.

With a sudden rush of fatigue, he realised it wasn't going to be easy. If these villagers were looking for them, others might be too.

CHAPTER TWENTY-SEVEN

Sweating and trembling, Duke strode casually back into the barn to find the others waiting for him.

'Well? How did it go?' Spike asked. 'It looked ok.'

'And they've gone off in the opposite direction,' said Billy. 'They must've believed you were the farmer.'

Meatball studied Duke's face. 'Something's wrong, isn't it?'

Duke's head began to shake. 'I didn't convince them, I know I didn't. The others maybe, but not that police sergeant.'

'But they walked away.'

'I know they did, but you should've seen the look he gave me. I did, or said something wrong: something the farmer doesn't normally do, I expect. We need to leave. Now.'

'You think he'll be back, then? The policeman?'

Duke nodded. 'I'm sure he will.'

They wasted no time in grabbing their things, sliding out of the doors, and down the side of the barn. Across the yard, they kept low to the ground, darting between the farm buildings until they came to the thick hedgerow running along the edge of the field.

Squeezing through a gap, they crawled along through the knee-high grass, thick with wild flowers. The air was alive with the gentle hum of bees. Butterflies crowded thirstily around the flowers, rising in a cloud as they pushed through.

'Once we get through that far hedge and into the other field, we can run for it,' Duke said. 'The station's about a mile beyond that. If we keep to the trees for as long as we can, we might just be able to get into the station without being seen.'

A spindly green grasshopper sprung nimbly into the air between Doc's fingers. 'Won't they be looking out for us?' 'That's where I'd be looking,' Billy said. 'They'll be watching places like that, I bet.'

'Never mind that,' Spike called back over his shoulder, 'we'll deal with that when we come to it …'

He had no time to finish: he had collided shoulder on with two slender legs. Swallowing hard, he looked down at a pair of scuffed brown shoes, and then up into the face of the farmer's wife.

'Well, now,' she said. 'I thought I saw you young'uns slipping out of that barn of ours. What you doing, playing round here?'

Spike knelt at her feet, staring up at her. 'We … um …'

'We're terribly sorry,' Terri said, standing up and walking towards her, 'we were hunting butterflies. And we know your field has all the best ones.'

'Is that right?' The farmer's wife lifted an eyebrow. 'Don't give me none of that old flannel,' she went on. 'I know what you lot are up to.'

Meatball, Duke and Spike stood up, forming a shield to hide Jophan and Neeza, who were keeping discreetly in the background.

'My word,' she said. 'You kids are getting big these days, aren't you? I don't think I've seen you round here before, have I? New to the village, are you?'

'Yes,' Doc piped up, 'we're staying with our grandma. Mum sent us here to stay with her because of the bombing. You know.'

'Your gran, you say?' She looked them up and down. 'Funny clothes they have in the city.' She suddenly snapped her fingers. 'Wait a bit, though, you wouldn't be old Mrs Tressell's grandchildren, would you? She said you was coming to stay.'

'That's right,' said Billy, brightly.

The farmer's wife looked down at him. 'Yes, you have got a look of her about you.' She put out a hand and patted his head. 'You're a nice lad, I can tell, but don't give me no nonsense about butterflies.'

She wagged a finger at them. 'I know what you're really up to,' she said. 'You're after some of them plums off my tree there, aren't you? Nice and ripe they are now.'

Her suntanned face broke into a smile. 'Go on then,' she said. 'You go and help yourself. Daresay you don't get a lot of fruit at home these days. You go and help yourself while I nip into the kitchen and see if I've got some nice biscuits.'

'Thank you very much,' Terri called, as the farmer's wife turned and walked away towards the kitchen.

As soon as she had disappeared through the doorway, they took off, running through the rest of the field, then into the field beyond.

'Where's the station?'

'It's over there somewhere, it's got to be.'

Spike bobbed up from behind the hedge. 'There's the church!' he cried, dropping down again. 'I can just see the steeple. The old station's just down the road from there. As long as we make for that steeple, we're bound to find it.'

Scrambling low to keep out of sight behind the hedgerow, they hurried on, keeping the steeple of St John's church in view. It was gradually getting nearer, yet still seemed far away: a tall, broad spire, almost glowing in the bright sunshine and visible for miles around.

Ten minutes later, they burst through the hedgerow and into the churchyard, slipped in and out of the gravestones, up the gravel path and out through the old wooden lichgate.

And there it was. The last piece of their journey. The road that would lead them to the station, and hopefully to home.

Only if the portal works, Spike said to himself, only if it exists here, in this time, and *only* if it works.

Running down the road beside the others, he tried not to think about that possibility, but it kept going round in his mind. What if there was no portal at the station? What if it had gone? What Terri had said was worrying too. What if she was right and it took them back to Gullivan?

Round and round in his mind like a bad dream … their only hope of getting back home.

He glanced ahead into the distance. There it was. Time to find out.

Darting into the cover of some bushes, they peered out at the old railway station and suddenly realised the time portal was only one of their worries. The old station wasn't the desolate run-down wreck of a place they had left in the present day. This was wartime, this was the main railway station and the whole place was alive with people. Passengers were arriving and waiting on platforms and porters were rushing here and there.

Terri gasped with dismay. 'Oh, please, no.'

'We forgot,' Doc said. 'It's not like in our time. This is the only railway station and there's going to be people everywhere.'

Meatball scrunched his fist into his hair. 'Damn it, why didn't we think of that?'

'We cannot think of everything,' said Jophan.

Spike shook his head in disbelief. Surely, nothing else could go wrong. 'Ok,' he said. 'Let's stay calm. How are we going to get in there without being seen?'

'Perhaps it'll be better if it's crowded,' said Billy. 'We can sneak past them and into the waiting room.'

'They'll be people in *there* too,' said Meatball. 'They'll see us.'

'They will see *us*,' said Jophan.

'We crowd together,' said Duke. 'Keep Jo and Neez in the centre. Make sure you keep your heads down, Jo. It's all we can do.'

Entering the station through a small side area where several bicycles stood propped against the wall, they walked as casually as they could up a long grey slope onto the platform.

It was even busier than they'd imagined: noisy and bustling. The air was full of sound, there was the general hum of conversation, occasional bursts of laughter, the cries of children and the calls of the staff and doors slamming.

Milk churns stood at the end of the platform. The sound of clucking chickens came from wooden crates stacked beside them. Piles of labelled boxes waited for despatch.

On another platform, a large hissing steam train was just pulling away, huge wheels shuddering and clanking, the stack belching black smoke.

Other platforms, Spike thought. Of course, there had been more than two platforms years ago.

Setting off toward the waiting room, they moved in a group close to the wall, Jo and Neeza shuffling along in the middle trying to stay hidden and their hoods pulled close to their faces.

Spike glanced across to the opposite platform and his heart dropped.

Soldiers.

Pull yourself together, he told himself, of course there'll be soldiers. This is wartime.

He felt the wave of tension run through them all. The others had seen them too, and he knew the same thought would be going through their minds. The police were looking for them. What if the soldiers also knew? What if they'd been told to look out for them?

Suddenly, ridiculously, every figure on the platform seemed to be staring at them. Every face seemed to have a threatening look.

Slowly moving on, they filtered through the crowd. A group of people clustered around the window of a small tearoom. Further down the platform in the distance was the waiting room.

Casually, they walked on, wanting to rush, but trying not to, all the while struggling to keep calm.

Maybe the soldiers wouldn't see them, Spike kept telling himself, maybe the soldiers wouldn't even know about them.

Carefully, they manoeuvred in and out of the passengers, who were now rising from their seats and moving toward the edge of the platform. A voice suddenly rose on the air.

'Platform 1, for the 9.37 to Broadgate, calling at Blackwater, Nutfield Common, Sedgewick Junction, Padsworth, Raynes Hill and all stations to Broadgate. Passengers for Coopers Halt, change at Sedgewick Junction. Please stand clear of the edge.'

Spike felt relief wash over him. If a train was coming in, it would shield them from view and the waiting room might empty.

Nervously, he glanced across at the opposite platform and breathed again. The soldiers had gone. He felt absurdly elated. Thank God.

'*Oi! You kids!*'

The voice echoed down the platform, mingling with the puffing of the approaching train.

They stopped and swung around. No wonder the soldiers had disappeared: they had slipped down into the connecting tunnel beneath and were now running up onto Platform 1.

'Stop! You kids there, stop! *Stop those children!*'

In a blind panic, they broke into a run, passengers scattering in all directions as they ploughed their way through. A woman let out a scream as Billy knocked her to one side, desperate to keep up with the others.

Turning, Spike grabbed him and yanked him along behind him. Ahead, the others kept running, no longer bothering to try to conceal Jophan and Neeza, who were running at full pelt, their hoods flying in the breeze.

A man cried out in alarm as Jophan ran past him. '*What in God's name?*'

But they didn't stop, they couldn't stop, even for a moment. The only thing that mattered was getting to the waiting room. In front, Duke saw two men put down their cases and stretch themselves across the platform in front of him to bar their way.

'Now, come on kids,' one was saying loudly. 'No use running. Whatever it is, it ain't the end of the world.'

Yes, it *is*, Spike's brain was screaming. It is! You don't know!

The next few moments were a blur of shouting soldiers, tramping boots, yelling passengers, screaming children, and their own pounding hearts. And above it all, the steadily increasing roar of the approaching steam train.

Then, suddenly, everything changed.

CHAPTER TWENTY-EIGHT

On the platform in front of them, the two men stretched out as far as they could, blocking their way. Behind, soldiers and station staff had slowed to a walk and were now advancing toward them, arms outstretched.

'Ain't nowhere to run, kids. We only want to talk to you.'

At that moment, from the base of the crystal hanging on the chain around Neeza's neck, a shaft of purple light poured forward, broke free from the crystal, and spread at lightning speed across the platform. From the ground to the roof, the light spread out to form a semi-transparent barrier between the children and everyone else on the station.

Yet again, there was no time to avoid it, no time for anyone to reach out for them before it closed in.

Rapidly spreading along the platform in all directions, it engulfed everything and everyone in its path - soldiers, porters, stationmaster, and passengers alike.

Those who had been watching and waiting froze in an instant, held tightly in its grasp.

Those who had been running toward them hung in the purple curtain as if in a spider's web, arms and legs stuck wildly in the air and faces contorted with shock and surprise.

Almost weeping with relief, Spike and the others watched, but only for a moment.

'It's *you* ...'

Meatball was staring along the platform at a spot just before the waiting room door, but this time it was different.

This time they, too, saw what Meatball could see. A young woman in a crisp uniform, her shining hair swept upwards from her forehead in a clip, atop a head of neat curls. They saw the bright red lips of her smiling face, and the twinkling blue eyes, the long, honey-coloured, slender legs, and gleaming black shoes.

'It's *you*,' Meatball said, again. He turned to face them. 'It's that woman again, the one I keep seeing.'

'We know,' Neeza whispered, placing a hand on his arm. 'We see her too.'

Billy gasped. 'Who *is* she?'

Meatball shook his head, solemnly, as if trying to shake an idea into his brain. 'I … I don't know … but I feel as if I should.'

The woman raised her hand and beckoned them onward, then melted slowly through the door of the waiting room.

Relief flooded over them all. Meatball's face creased into a smile. 'I think we're going home,' he said.

Moving towards the door, he reached out and opened it and they stepped inside. Three people sat on the long wooden benches against the wall: three people now frozen, as if suspended in time, but there was no one else. Their guardian angel had vanished.

'She's gone again,' Meatball said, frustration and sorrow in his voice. 'She's gone again, and I didn't get the chance to talk to her or thank her.'

'This is it!' cried Billy. 'Look! It's the picture! The one that was there before!'

Jophan walked across to put his hand in the centre. He nodded. 'Yes, this is the one: the energy field is here.'

As they watched, the steam train in the picture puffed slowly into the tunnel and out the other end. This time it didn't stop but simply continued on its way off around the side of the hill, puffing out a huge cloud of smoke as it disappeared into the distance.

They watched it in wonder.

'It's almost as if it's saying, 'Job Done,' Duke said. With a deep breath, he walked across the waiting room to the other door and gripped the handle. 'Oh, well. Here goes nothing. Come on.'

Together, they walked through the door … and straight into the waiting room.

'*What*?'

They whirled around to stare at the waiting room door behind them.

'This can't be right. We've just left the waiting room. How can we still be in it?'

Doc stood in the middle of the waiting room, gazing around in wonder. A smile lit up her face. 'We're *not*,' she said. 'Look around you. There's no-one here. Everything's old and faded and covered in dust.'

'We're *back*,' said Terri, biting back a sob. She walked across to the window, pulling her coat tightly around her. 'Look outside at that lovely snow.'

'Oh … *yes*,' Spike breathed.

Meatball let out a long, tremulous sigh. 'Let's go home.'

'Wait.' Billy darted across to the window. 'What was that?'

'What?'

He spun around to look at them. 'Didn't you see it? Something outside the window?'

Terri leaned over to look. 'What was it, Bill? What did you see?'

'Out there.' He pointed through the window. 'There was someone out there, peering in. I'm sure there was.'

Spike walked to the door and pulled it open. 'There's no one here, Bill.'

Meatball pushed through and stood on the snowy platform. 'It wasn't the lady again, was it?'

Please don't let it be her, Spike thought. He felt ungrateful saying it, but if she was still around, it could only mean one thing: they weren't home at all, and if they weren't, they were here for another reason. A feeling of guilt washed over him. After all she'd done for them, he was wishing her away.

Billy shook his head. 'No,' he said, 'it wasn't her. I'm sure it wasn't.'

Spike looked up and down the platform. 'Well, whoever it was has gone,' he said, firmly.

He followed Meatball back into the waiting room, rubbing his hands together. 'It's freezing out there.'

Meatball grinned. 'Yeah. Great, isn't it?'

Duke was over by the picture. 'Probably just a trick of the light,' he said. 'The picture's still here, but it's kind of dead. Look.'

The picture was lifeless, the colours faded and worn. Jo put his hand in the centre. 'It is gone. The energy field is no longer present.'

'We *are* home,' said Neeza, joyfully. 'I feel it.'

Tears welled in Terri's eyes. She gulped to hold back the tears and at that moment, the door behind them smashed open with a thunderous crash against the wall.

Stupefied with horror, Spike watched as two figures stumbled in through the doorway. They were figures he knew only too well. The first, who was taller, lean and scrawny, had his arm tightly around the throat of a boy and was now dragging him towards the bench, where he almost collapsed onto the seat.

Cornelius Gullivan was shivering violently, yet wet with sweat, his face pale and corpse-like. His left shoulder was soaked with blood. In his left hand, he somehow held a knife and it pointed in the direction of the boy's throat.

Beneath his right arm, Brett Tyler struggled desperately, pulling at the arm that held him fast and tears running down his face. '*Help me ...*'

'Shut it!'

Gullivan's voice was feeble and hoarse: his breathing laboured and evidently painful. With some effort, he growled, '*YOU!* You! Girl! Get over 'ere!'

He nodded towards Doc. The others stepped toward her, protectively.

'*GET OVER HERE NOW, GIRL AND HEAL MY SHOULDER!*'

178

The roar had taken all his strength. His head drooped with the effort. Brett Tyler struggled and Gullivan's arm tightened about him. 'I know you can do it!' he snapped. 'I know all about that soldier! Now, get over 'ere, or the boy here gets my knife!'

He moved the blade of the knife closer to Brett's face. Brett let out a long squeal.

Doc looked at Brett's face, twisted with terror and wet with tears. 'No!' she cried. 'No, don't hurt him! I'll do it!' She moved toward him. The others immediately followed.

'Not you lot!' Gullivan snapped. 'You stay where you are!'

Reluctantly, Terri let go of Doc's arm.

Doc looked at them all, nodded and then walked across to stand beside Gullivan. Being so close to him, the look on Doc's face said everything. Clearly, the sight and smell of him made her want to retch. She lingered for a moment, just staring at him.

'Get on with it!' he screamed.

Reaching out, Doc tugged at the material on his shoulder. He let out a bellow of pain. '*Aagh!*' he roared. '*You ...*'

The sudden holler made Doc jump with shock. She stopped, just staring at him, as if she was remembering everything this man was responsible for. Every threat, every menacing look, everyone he'd hurt. Everything he had done seemed to be welling up inside her. She swayed slightly, weak with fatigue and tiredness, and then she stood up straight, hands on hips, as though her fear had washed away from her in a wave.

Leaning closer, she screamed in his face. '*D'YOU WANT ME TO HELP YOU OR NOT?*'

For a few moments there was a deafening silence. Brett's jaw hung open. Behind her, the others held their breath.

Spike stared at Doc. She was tiny, what was she doing? He hated Gullivan, but he wasn't sure he could stand up to him like that.

Gullivan forced his head around to look at her and then gripped the knife. 'Just get on with it,' he spat.

Doc took a step backward. 'Let him go,' she said.

He glared at her, anger and pain burning in his eyes. Slowly, he pushed the knife closer to Brett's throat.

'Fix my shoulder,' he growled, 'or I'll fix him.'

Brett let out another squeal.

Doc crossed her arms. 'I'll heal your shoulder,' she said, defiantly, 'when you've let him go.'

'Oh yeah?' Gullivan's voice was failing. 'What d'you think I am? Stupi …?'

He broke off. His head drooped again. Weak from loss of blood, he slumped back against the bench.

With a sudden burst, Brett broke free from his grip, slithered away like a snake, and bolted out of the door.

Moving forward, Doc held her hands over Gullivan's shattered shoulder.

'What are you doing, Doc? You don't have to do this!'

Doc gave Spike a quick glance. 'I cannot choose.'

She continued with the healing. Despite their fear, they watched, transfixed, as the wound released the bullet, the shattered bones reformed and the lacerated flesh began to knit.

Gullivan's body shivered with release and he let out a long sigh.

His mouth opened slightly and it crossed Spike's mind that Gullivan might be going to thank her, but he said nothing. His hand reached up to rub his shoulder, now whole and clean, and then, rising swiftly to his feet, he pushed them roughly aside and stepped out through the other door.

Through the window, they watched him stop short and look wildly around, then run up and down the platform, as if searching, checking now and then to look behind him.

'I suspect he is looking for the time portal,' said Jophan. 'He seeks to escape. He has a haunted look like one who is fearful.'

'I wonder who he's afraid of?'

As Billy spoke, the front door smashed open for a second time, crashing into the wall, and a man blundered into the room. It was the same man they'd seen in the village, but this time he was alone. The huge, spiky-haired dog wasn't with him. His hair was wet and dripping snow. On his head, a wound trickled blood down onto his reddened cheek. The man's hand, reaching into the inside pocket of his jacket, froze for a moment when he saw them, then it relaxed and moved slowly back to his side.

Filled with a sudden foreboding, Spike's hand moved in his own pocket to check for the outline of Billy's knife. The hairs on the back of his neck stood up. Here was a man who had chatted to them quite casually about his dog, but for some reason he felt uneasy.

The others, too, had an automatic distrust of the man without knowing why, the same intuitive dislike they'd felt for the gangsters the year before. Instinctively, Jo and Neeza pulled up their hoods and moved to stand behind the others.

Adopting a carefree, cheery manner, the man said, 'Hallo again, kids. I don't suppose you've seen a man about? Tall and gangly, looks as though he could do with a good wash. He was supposed to be meeting me here.'

'You mean Gullivan?' Spike muttered.

The man's eyes narrowed. 'You know him?'

'Yeah,' said Duke. 'We know him. And he just ran out of that door.'

With a sudden burst of speed, Toby McKendrick bolted for the door and ran out onto the platform.

CHAPTER TWENTY-NINE

This couldn't be right ... this could not be *right*!
Hysterically, Gullivan ran up and down the empty
platform. Where was it? Where was the damned time portal?
He stopped for a moment, trying to clear his head. Steady,
he told himself. Keep calm. Think.
*The door! Of course, you damned fool! You've come out
of the wrong door!*
Joy surging in his heart, he turned and ran back to the door
of the waiting room. In a couple of minutes, he'd be out the
other side and into Roman Britain and McKendrick could rot
in hell.
As his hand reached out for the handle, he heard a crash.
Moving across to the window, he peered stealthily around
the very edge and almost collapsed where he stood.
Toby McKendrick had just burst into the waiting room
and was now talking to the kids.
Swinging around, Gullivan stared hard into the distance
through the first swirling flakes of yet another heavy
snowfall. Further up the line, he could just make out the
beginning of a tunnel. If he could get there before
McKendrick got to him ...
Running down the slope at the end of the platform, he
turned towards the tunnel and ran for his life.

CHAPTER THIRTY

Inside the waiting room, Spike and the others watched through the window as the man burst outside and onto the platform.

The man was looking wildly up and down and then, as if he had glimpsed something in the distance, he ran down the platform and into the snow.

'I wonder what he wants with Gullivan?' Meatball whispered.

Walking to the door, Duke twisted the brass handle and peered outside. 'I don't know,' he said. 'But I'm glad it's not me he's after. He was carrying a gun. Did you see his hand reaching into his pocket?'

Venturing out onto the snowy platform, they saw Cornelius Gullivan in the distance, staggering as fast as he could through the snow towards the dark mouth of a tunnel.

Still some distance behind, the man from the waiting room bounded after him. They saw him stop, pull the gun from his jacket, raise it into the air and take aim.

Through the crisp icy air, they heard angry shouts, but after a moment the man lowered the gun.

'I think he's just realised Gullivan's too far off,' Duke hissed. 'He'll never hit him from there. Not through this snow.'

'And Gullivan's gone into the tunnel now!'

'No point in risking anyone seeing, either,' Billy said. 'Not when he can kill him inside the tunnel.'

'It seems likely that was the man who shot Gullivan before,' said Neeza, as they watched the figure with the gun stagger toward the opening.

Jophan nodded. 'This man is the cause of Gullivan's fear, I think.'

'D'you think we ought to tell someone?' Doc said.

Spike looked at her. 'Nope,' he said.

'But …' Terri stopped. 'What's that? Over there, by the mouth of the tunnel?'

It was a light. Not a headlight. Not like the light from a lamp carried by a man, or even the radiant purple shimmer of a time portal entrance. This light was gleaming gold, fringed with brilliant orange and crimson red, like fire: this light filled the tunnel entrance, pulsing like the mouth of a fiery furnace.

Through the snowflakes, Spike and the others saw the figure with the gun slow to a jog, stop, and then spinning around, start lumbering across the snow in the opposite direction.

'Something's spooked him …'

'What is it that he sees?' gasped Jophan.

'It's a train,' said Meatball.

'A *train*?'

'It can't be,' Duke said, slowly. 'It can't be a train.' He stared ahead through the snow. 'It can't be, can it? Not now. Not in our time. This station hasn't been used since the sixties.'

'It can't be!' Doc caught her breath. 'There's no track!

'This isn't a normal train.'

'What do you mean, Meatball?'

Meatball shook his head. 'I mean it's not normal, Terri. It's like some*one's* coming, not some*thing* … a presence … and there's nothing good about it …'

Neeza stepped back. 'We should be afraid, Jo. I feel it.'

Jo stepped toward her. 'We must …'

But there was no more time.

Before he could finish, an enormous steam train exploded from the mouth of the tunnel like a launched missile.

Terri let out a scream of shock.

Rooted to the spot with terror they gasped and cried out as the gigantic engine thundered towards them, black, gleaming and radiating menace.

'What the hell is that?!' Spike shrieked as the huge wheels sliced through the snowstorm, spinning towards them in a blast of light.

'It's massive!' Duke yelled.

'That's not a train!' Meatball cried. 'I told you! That thing's evil! Quick!'

Doc started screeching hysterically as the engine soared towards them. Body glistening and pistons pumping, it reared up in a roar of glowing fire. Crimson smoke belched from the engine's funnel in a continuous stream, crackling and sparking like blazing fireworks.

In seconds, the terrifying spectre was upon them, hissing and snorting, like some fearsome animal hunting in the night.

Battered by the shockwave of pulsing heat and fiery embers, they tumbled backwards against the station wall, staring into the monstrous black carriages as they thundered past, heads reeling from the terrifying roar of the wheels. As the platform rumbled beneath them, they slid down onto the concrete overwhelmed by the scorching heat, watching through half closed eyes as the train flew into the distance.

In seconds, it had melted through the snowy hillside, and vanished from view, leaving no sign of disturbance in the snow, except for a slight echoing in the air, which rang in their heads for a moment, leaving a trail of emptiness.

Sitting haphazardly on the icy platform, they moved closer together. Inexplicably, Spike felt on the edge of despair, suddenly wanting and needing more than ever to be home.

Over on the hillside, no sight of the ghostly train remained. The snowflakes were slowing and thinning.

Terri covered her face with her hands and cried. 'What *was* that?' She hugged Doc, who had buried her head in Terri's coat, muffling yet another sob.

Shaking, Spike's eyes brimmed with tears and he swallowed to quell the sheer terror he'd felt as the ghostly

185

apparition had soared past. He reached out for Billy, whose tears were already rolling down his face, and slipped a protective arm about his shoulders.

Neeza sat close to Jo, eyes shut tight, each comforting the other.

Still trembling, Duke bit back more tears. 'What was that? *What was it?*'

Meatball wiped his face roughly with his sleeve. 'Better we don't know,' he snapped, gruffly.

In the watery snowflakes, they huddled together for a few moments and then got jerkily to their feet.

Billy gripped Spike's arm. 'Spike! What about Gullivan? He was in that tunnel, wasn't he? What about him? Where's he gone?'

'But he was *in* there!' Neeza cried. 'Did you not see him? He was *in there!*'

They looked back at the tunnel now just an ice cold, black semicircle draped in snow.

Neeza put her hands to her cheeks. 'Mr Gullivan,' she said. '*Mr Gullivan was in the train!*'

'What? Driving it, you mean?'

'No!' she cried. 'Inside! He was trapped inside! Did you not see him?'

They shook their heads.

'You are sure of this, Neez?'

Neeza fixed her brother with a long look. 'I am not mistaken,' she said.

'Gullivan?' Doc gasped. 'Trapped inside *that* thing?'

'What do we do now?' asked Terri.

'Do?' Wiping his nose on his sleeve, Spike pulled his hoodie tightly about him. 'I don't know about you lot,' he said, 'but I'm going home.'

'Good idea,' said Meatball.

'What about him?'

Billy pointed over in the distance to where the figure with the gun lay in the snow.

'He couldn't have been hit by the train,' Duke said. 'He was running away.'

'Perhaps he's fainted,' said Terri.

'Perhaps I ought to help him,' Doc said, vaguely.

As she spoke, the figure in the snow sat up. He sat still for a while as if trying to recover his senses, and then he slowly stood up, swayed a little, righted himself and trudged off.

'Don't suppose we'll see him round here again,' Terri said, quietly. 'Not now Gullivan's gone. Unless he's moved in somewhere in the village.'

Together, they stepped out of the waiting room and set off for home.

'He doesn't look like a local,' said Spike. 'Doesn't sound like one, either. We'll ask Gran. She might know.'

Jophan stopped suddenly. A mobile phone lay in the snow before him. He stooped to pick it up.

'Hello, whose is this?' Spike switched it on. It went straight to Brett's Photos. 'Hold on a minute ... so *that's* what he was doing at the waiting room. There's photos of us on here, and photos of Jo and Neeza! The slimy ...'

'It must've been him I saw at the window!' Billy cried. 'He must have run into Gullivan just after.'

'Yes, and now we know who Gullivan was running away from. He must've been hoping to escape through the time portal.'

'And then out of the blue, we appear,' said Spike.

'And he sees me,' Doc said, with a shudder.

Neeza chuckled. 'But not the Doc he was expecting, I think.'

'Standing up to him like that took some guts, Doc. Even though he was wounded,' Terri said.

The others nodded in admiration.

'If I'd stopped to think about it, I probably wouldn't have done it,' she said. 'But I suppose something inside me just snapped.'

'Don't know why you bargained for Brett's life like that, though,' Spike muttered. 'I'd have left him to it.'

Terri gave him a sideways glance. 'No you wouldn't, Spike.'

'Yes, I would. I hate him.'

'With good reason,' said Meatball. 'But I s'pose we probably would've helped him. We couldn't have left him with that murderer, could we?'

'Served him right,' said Duke. 'He must've been hanging about the station since we disappeared.'

Probably thought we were hiding out somewhere.'

'We were,' said Terri, remembering. 'In Roman Britain.'

Crossing the road, they made their way across the car park and back down to the village.

'We must hope we do not meet with Brett Tyler again,' said Neeza.

'Brett Tyler is a bully and a coward,' Jophan declared.

'He won't be out now,' Spike said. 'If I know Tyler, he's run home screaming to mummy.'

Billy looked thoughtful. 'What if he goes to the police?'

'Then he does,' said Meatball. 'What's he going to tell them?'

'Yet it would be advisable, I think, to keep out of sight as much as possible,' said Jophan.

He pulled tightly on his hood, lifting the scarf that shielded much of his face. 'He may indeed go to the authorities and they may come looking. It would be disastrous if, after all we have been through, we were now to be discovered.'

Duke nodded. 'Jo's right. We mustn't let our guard down, not till we get back to your gran's.'

CHAPTER THIRTY-ONE

The door at Yew Tree Cottage opened before any of them could touch the handle.

Swinging gently on its hinges, the heavy oak door opened onto the long polished hallway, full of welcoming sounds and smells.

At the end, waiting for them with relief and pride etched on their faces, stood Gran and Mr Price.

'*Gran!*' Billy was the first to break away from the group and run into Gran's welcoming embrace.

'My dears! Welcome home! Come in all of you, there's a lovely warm fire in the kitchen. Let's get you fed and rested and later you can tell us all your news!'

Spike threw his arms around her. 'Oh Gran,' he said. 'Tell me that's steak and kidney pie I can smell?'

She laughed. 'It is.'

Meatball punched the air. '*Yes!*'

'Bring it on,' Duke said.

Terri trembled with relief. Next to her, Doc swayed slightly.

Gran moved at once to her side and slipped an arm about her. 'You need to rest, my dear. Come and sit by the fire.'

Behind her, Mr Price put a hand on the shoulders of Jo and Neeza. 'Come along in,' he said. 'There's a very special visitor waiting to see you.'

A tall, aristocratic figure appeared. With a bound of joy, Neeza ran to him.

'*Father!*' Rushing toward him, Jo threw himself into his father's arms.

'My children! And all of you! I am so relieved to see you all.'

His arms still wrapped around his children, Arisius looked across at the others, now settled in the centre of a large ring of cosy chairs that surrounded the fire. 'No doubt you all have a great deal to tell us, but first you must rest and eat. There is time enough to hear your news.'

They needed no persuasion. Exhausted, cold and hungry, they all sat together and tucked into the food until they could eat no more and then sank back into the soft chairs.

In the peace and safety of Yew Tree Cottage, they surrendered to the warmth of the fire and relaxed into peaceful sleep.

Several hours passed, and when they woke, the brightness of day was beginning to dim.

With a long stretch, Spike sat up. Beside him, Billy dozed peacefully. In chairs opposite, the others sprawled in deep sleep. Only Terri was awake, resting and staring ahead of her into the glowing embers of the fire.

'You all right, Terri?'

Terri eased her head around to look at him and nodded slowly. 'Fine,' she said. 'Can't sleep.'

'Thinking about stuff?'

She nodded again. 'All seems like a dream now, doesn't it?'

Spike nodded.

'Maybe it was,' said Billy, rousing himself.

'What d'you mean, Bill?'

Billy shrugged. 'Nothing.'

'Let's go and find Gran,' said Spike, pushing himself carefully to his feet, 'see if there's anything to eat.'

'*Eat*?' Terri looked at him, aghast. 'After the lot you've just scoffed?'

'Always room for a bit more,' said Meatball. He yawned so wide it almost engulfed his face.

'If there's any grub going, it's mine,' Duke murmured, eyes still closed.

Terri looked across at Doc: fast asleep, still exhausted.

'She's shattered,' she said.

Duke nodded. 'Yeah. Must be that healing stuff. Wait a minute ... where's Jo and Neeza? Surely, they wouldn't have left without saying goodbye?'

They got up and walked outside into the kitchen. Jophan and Neeza were there, sitting in chairs beside their father, talking.

'I'm so glad you're still here,' Terri said, to Neeza. 'For a horrible moment, I thought you might have had to leave.'

'We would never leave without saying goodbye,' said Arisius. 'Besides, we have yet to hear of your adventures.'

'We've only just woken up too,' Neeza explained.

'Yes, and we have said nothing as yet,' Jo said. 'We were waiting for you.' He glanced around. 'Doc still sleeps?'

Duke nodded. 'We'll wait until she wakes up.'

'I'm up,' said a voice from the doorway. 'Sorry, guys, have you been waiting for me?' Doc stepped into the kitchen, stifling a yawn. 'Oh dear ... I was so tired.'

'Not surprised after that lot,' Spike said.

There was a short silence.

'Start at the beginning,' Joseph Price said, encouragingly.

A confusion of voices followed.

'Maybe,' Arisius interrupted, 'elect one of you to speak, and the others contribute to the story as it progresses.'

Duke felt eyes staring at him.

'Go on, Duke,' said Spike. 'You're best at all that.'

'Yeah, Duke, you do it,' said Meatball, nodding. 'You're good at that sort of stuff.'

'Tell us everything,' Joseph said, 'we know very little as yet.'

Duke shrugged. 'Ok,' he said,' but I might miss bits. You'll have to help me.' He took a breath. 'I guess,' he said, thoughtfully, 'it all started at the fair ...'

He began to relate the entire story. The purple sign they'd seen on the notice board and the other strange signs, the new skills they had suddenly acquired, their suspicions about Gullivan, their encounters with Brett Tyler and his gang, and their timeslip into Roman Britain.

Joseph Price muttered. 'Roman Britain! So that's where that revolting creature has been hiding.'

'As if you didn't know,' Gran said, quietly. 'Continue, my loves.'

Duke described their trip to the research establishment, Meatball's vision, and their strange and unexpected escape.

'When we realised where we were, we couldn't believe it!' said Billy, breathlessly. 'The Second World War, Gran! We were actually there, in the war!'

Gran put down the teapot and leaned on the table. 'And this lady, the one you saw in your vision, Meatball. You say you recognised her?'

Meatball shook his head, sadly, staring at the table as though trying to see through a fog. 'No,' he said. 'But I feel as though I ought to have done. As though somehow I knew her.' He held up his hands in a hopeless gesture. 'But I don't know who she *is.*'

'Don't bother it,' said Mr Price, softly. 'It'll turn up. You'll know when the time is right.'

Duke continued with the story, helped at intervals with snippets of information from the others. Another mention of Cornelius Gullivan brought a frown to Mr Price's face.

'He is a perpetual thorn in the side, that one.'

'A thorn?' Gran scoffed. 'More like a rusty blade.'

'It would seem,' Arisius said, gravely, 'that Cornelius Gullivan is even more dangerous than we had supposed. One cannot help but consider what possible purpose he can serve.'

'Cornelius Gullivan must never be underestimated,' said Gran, soberly. 'There is method in his madness.'

'Fortunately, he is not without his own enemies,' Joseph interrupted. 'Continue, Duke.'

Duke took a deep breath. 'Well, like Bill says, there we were in the war. But we realised fairly quickly that we were at home, too.'

'Home?'

'Yep, we were here, Gran. In the village,' said Spike. 'We recognised it.'

'We were in the right *place*,' Doc said. 'Just the wrong time.'

'And that was merely the beginning,' said Jophan.

'Your work, I assume, was not yet finished,' murmured Joseph.

Duke looked at him. 'No,' he said. 'As it happens, it was far from finished.'

He told them of the aeroplane and the shop, of the young couple and the pilot and of how they found themselves at the farm, then the station and all its problems, and how, but for each of their particular abilities, they may not have made it back to the present day.

And when the story was finally finished, Duke sat back, hardly able to believe it himself. 'It all seems like ...'

'A dream?' Joseph suggested.

'That's what I said,' Billy piped up. 'It all seems like a dream. Only it wasn't. It couldn't have been, could it? It was real. As real as sitting here.'

'It was most certainly real,' said Gran. 'And you accomplished the tasks you were set with great courage. You assumed when you found yourselves in the war, that there was a reason and you were correct.'

'Everything happens for a reason,' said Joseph.

Doc looked up. 'We were meant to save those people, then? The young couple in the shop, and the pilot? We were there specifically to save them?'

'That, too, was part of our mission?' Neeza asked.

Joseph nodded. 'Exactly.'

A loud ring of the doorbell echoed down the hallway. Joseph rose from his seat.

'Aha!' he said. 'I do believe that's our visitor.'

CHAPTER THIRTY-TWO

In the kitchen of Yew Tree Cottage, Spike and the others waited with baited breath as Joseph Price walked out into the hall.

In his chair, Spike felt tense. A visitor, he thought? A stranger? What was Mr Price doing? Had he forgotten Jo and Neeza were in the room? And Arisius?

He listened to the sound of footsteps up the hall and the opening of the door, then a few exchanged words. Perhaps, whoever it was, he wasn't going to bring them in.

Moments later, Joseph reappeared in the doorway. 'We have a visitor,' he announced. 'Someone who's very anxious to meet you all.'

He stood aside and an elderly man stepped into the room. Warmly dressed in a thick woollen jumper, he was frail and stooped, with neatly combed grey hair and lively blue eyes.

Duke recognised him at once. It was Henry Judd, the elderly curator of the local museum who had helped them with information about the railway lines.

Gran stepped forward to greet him.

'Mr Judd,' she said, 'how lovely to see you. Do, please, have a seat with us. I'll get you a nice hot cup of tea.'

Henry Judd inclined his head. 'Thank you. You are most kind.'

He stood for a long moment, staring at the children, scrutinising each of their faces. Then he looked last and longest at Jophan.

Standing up, Arisius stepped toward him and extended his hand. 'Mr Judd, allow me to introduce myself. I am Arisius, Jophan and Neeza's father. It is an honour and a privilege to make your acquaintance.'

Henry shook his hand warmly. A broad smile lit up his face. 'The honour is mine, sir, I assure you,' he said. His eyes were wet with tears. 'I knew it! I knew I was not mistaken! I knew I hadn't imagined it!'

Duke stepped forward. 'Mr Judd ... I'm Duke. You may remember us? You very kindly helped us at the museum?' 'Of course,' said Henry, shaking his hand. 'The information ... it was of some use, I hope?'

'It was just what we needed,' said Doc, brightly.

Walking around the table, Billy stepped forward and looked at Henry Judd.

'I'm Billy, Mr Judd,' he said. 'And I think I know who *you* are. You're the pilot, aren't you? The one we rescued from the tree?'

Henry stared at him, his eyes glistening with tears. 'I am!'

Spike's mouth dropped open. 'Wow!'

'That's amazing!' Terri cried.

'It's wonderful,' Doc breathed. 'But, surely ...?'

Henry smiled at her. 'Born to fly, I was. Top in the squadron. I wasn't quite truthful about my age, of course, along with one or two others, but they didn't seem to care much by that time.'

Jophan and Neeza approached Henry Judd, and bowed. 'My sister and I are honoured to meet you, sir.'

Henry took both their hands in his. 'I am honoured to meet you both,' he said. He looked up at Jophan. 'I *told* them,' he said. 'I told them all, but they wouldn't believe me. Delusions, they said. I was having delusions. I'd obviously sustained a head injury. But I knew I'd seen you, *I knew.*'

His eyes welled again. 'And to think I should have the opportunity to meet you!' He looked around. 'To meet you *all*. I am doubly blessed. If only my poor, dear Mary were alive to see this.' He glanced back at Joseph Price. 'She was the only one, you know, the only one who believed me.'

He paused for a moment, overcome with emotion. Looking at the children, he said, 'It doesn't matter, you see. It doesn't matter, when you *know*. There are times in your life when you experience something, when you see or feel something, and no one believes you. But it doesn't matter. It doesn't matter what anyone else says or believes, because you *know*.'

Slightly breathless, he leaned back in the chair beside them and accepted a cup of tea. 'And then of course, there's *these* …'

He glanced up at Joseph Price, who reached behind a chair to pull out a large bag.

'I never showed them to anyone,' Henry Judd continued, 'because as far as I was concerned, they didn't deserve to know. I showed them to no one except my dear Mary and she cherished them. She kept them most carefully.'

Joseph passed the bag across to the children. Stepping forward, Billy leaned in to look inside. His face lit up. 'Your coat, Spike! And my scarf!'

Spike took the coat and held it up. 'Look at that!' he cried. 'I've got a coat from the war! Thanks, Mr Judd!'

Everyone laughed.

'No,' said Henry Judd. 'Thank *you*. Both of you.' He looked around. '*All* of you. There are so many questions.' He smiled. 'But I ask none. It is sufficient that you bless me with this meeting. You have my absolute discretion …'

He raised his head to look steadily at Arisius. 'And my word.'

Arisius bowed. 'I thank you.'

With a trembling hand, Henry Judd lifted his cup and took a restorative sip or two of his tea, and then suddenly he lowered his cup with a bang onto the table, and said, 'Oh, my goodness! I must beg your forgiveness, what must you think of me? I've neglected to thank you for saving my life!'

His head shook slowly from side to side. 'I dread to think … if you hadn't helped me …'

Duke was the first to speak. 'It was our pleasure, Mr Judd. We are all very glad we could help, but it's really Doc you should thank.' He looked across at Doc. 'It was she who saved your life.'

'No, no, it wasn't just me,' Doc protested. 'Really, it was all of us.'

Reaching across the table, Henry Judd took Doc's hand and wrapped it in both of his.

'My dear,' he said. 'I can never repay you for saving my life. I can only thank you from the bottom of my heart. Without your help, I wouldn't have had all these wonderful years.'

Doc felt a warm glow of happiness. 'You're very welcome,' she croaked.

For a few moments, everyone was quiet.

'Now then,' Gran said, brightly. 'Who's for cake?'

It was two hours later, and after many goodbyes, Henry Judd had finally left, ferried to his home by Joseph Price.

Soon, Arisius announced that they, too, would have to leave and, with a heavy heart, they said farewell to their friends for a second time. Terri and Doc hugged Neeza tightly, holding their breath in an attempt to stop the tears.

'We will see you all again.' Jophan turned to his father. 'We will, won't we, Father?'

'A friendship as special as yours? Of course.'

Gran slipped her arms about Jo and Neeza's shoulders and held them tight. 'Have no fear, my dears. You are destined to meet again.'

Over at the doorway, the frame began to glow.

'Time to leave,' said Arisius, gently. 'Your mother is anxious to see you.'

With a final wave, they stepped through the purple doorway.

Spike and the others watched as the doorway rolled in around them. For a second or two, they could see them waving and then their friends were gone.

In the sudden silence that followed, Spike and the others stared at the doorway as if staring hard enough might make it open again.

But it didn't. The purple gateway merely collapsed to a tiny dot and then disappeared completely.

'That's it, then,' Doc said. 'They're gone.'

'I'm going to miss them,' said Duke. 'Got used to them being around.'

'And me.'

'Yeah.'

Terri heaved a long sigh. 'I wonder how long it'll be before we see them again?'

'That's enough, now,' said Gran, briskly, 'You probably ought to think about getting some proper rest. Put a film on or something.'

'Don't think so, Gran,' Spike said, yawning, 'a film would be a bit boring.'

It was dark outside now and the first few flakes of another snowy night were fluttering through the air like soft white butterflies.

'I've phoned your parents,' Gran said, cheerfully. 'I've told them you're staying the night here with Spike and Billy.'

'Thank you, Mrs Makepeace,' Terri said, politely. 'After everything that's happened, I don't feel quite ready to go home yet.'

'Nor do I,' said Meatball. 'All I keep seeing is the vision of the woman who helped us. Who was she?'

'Mr Price said you'll find out when it's time,' said Doc.

'Yeah, I know, and I suppose he's right as he usually is. But I just can't get rid of this feeling that I ought to know her. I mean, how can you recognise someone you don't know? It's not possible, is it?'

'Perhaps it's one of those experience things Mr Judd talked about,' said Spike. 'He said it doesn't matter, because you know.'

'Well, I don't,' said Meatball, miserably, 'and despite what Mr Price says, maybe I never will.'

Standing over by the window, watching the snowflakes, Duke was also deep in thought. 'Wonder what Brett Tyler's doing?' he said. 'D'you reckon he's all right after that business with Gullivan?'

'Yeah, course,' said Spike. 'That moron's always all right. If he fell off a cliff, he'd land on his feet.'

Terri pulled a face. 'That's hardly likely, is it.'

He chuckled. 'You know what I mean.'

'Brett Tyler bothers you that much?'

Joseph Price was back and slipping off his coat. 'You know,' he said, accepting a cup of tea from Gran, 'You shouldn't let Brett Tyler get under your skin.'

Spike pulled a face. 'I hate him.'

'So do I!' said Billy.

'Hatred and anger are negative emotions,' said Joseph. 'It will only make you weaker.'

'Not any more it won't,' said Spike, cheerfully. 'Not now I've got my super-strength.' He smacked his fist into his other hand. 'Next time he comes near me, I'll ...'

Gran looked across at Joseph. 'I'm afraid it doesn't quite work like that,' she said.

Spike let his hands drop to his sides. 'How d'you mean? Haven't we got our special skills anymore?' He clenched his fist and felt the reassuring strength in his hands.

'Yes, you still have them. You all do, they're lifelong, but you mustn't use them at other times.'

'Why not?'

Joseph leaned across to pat him on the shoulder. 'Think about it. If other people knew what *you* know. Think about what could happen. It may be difficult and heaven knows, Brett Tyler would try the patience of a saint, but that's a burden he has to bear. D'you see? You mustn't use your skills for any other purpose however much you are tempted.'

'And there is your own safety to consider too,' said Gran. 'If other people know of your particular talents, your lives will be changed forever. Some may even wish to harm you.'

'We understand, Gran,' said Billy. 'Not that it makes any difference for me.' He looked dolefully down at the fire. 'I haven't got anything anyway.'

'It's only because you're young, Bill,' said Spike, trying to comfort him. 'That's right, isn't it, Gran?'

'Well … in *part*,' Gran replied. She sat down beside him. 'But in your particular case, Billy, age is not a factor.'

Billy looked up at her. 'What d'you mean?'

'You're really smart, Bill,' said Terri. 'I bet that's it, isn't it?'

Gran smiled. 'In *part*,' she said. 'You are extremely intelligent, Billy, very good at seeing things clearly. You have a concise, logical mind, and in your next mission, your skill may be vital.'

'*It will*?'

'Oh, yes,' she said.

'Never underestimate your ability,' Joseph said. 'You may yet outshine us all.'

Spike patted him on the back. '*Wow*, Bill!'

'See, Bill?' Meatball grinned. 'Told you. Said you had more brains than Spike and Duke.'

They both turned to give him a look. 'Yeah, all right. He's got more brains than you, n'all.'

Doc laughed aloud. 'You've probably got more intelligence than all of us, Bill. Even Gus.'

'I wouldn't go that far,' said Meatball. 'Gus is quite clearly a genius. Just because he can't tell us, doesn't mean he isn't thinking genius stuff.'

Spike thought about Gus for a moment.

'He's a wicked cat,' he said, dreamily. 'You're so lucky, Meatball.'

'He's not just my cat,' Meatball, said with a smile. 'He's *our* cat. He's one of the team, now.'

Spike looked across at Ed's picture on the shelf above the fire. Suddenly, he missed him terribly and his heart ached.

'Yeah,' he said. 'He's one of the team.'

CHAPTER THIRTY-THREE

It was another ten days before the thaw set in. Ten whole days of snow flurries and blustery winds and temperatures that froze pipes, cracked guttering and topped the village pond with a thick white crust of ice.

That morning, as Spike and Billy looked out of their bedroom window, it was like being in a prison cell. Enormous long fingers of ice hung down from the roof past their window like bars. In the morning sun, drops of icy water ran down them to drip, drip, drip onto the snow below.

Spike looked at his watch. Almost nine o'clock. 'We'd better hurry up, Bill.'

'What time are we meeting the others?'

'Ten. But I promised Gran we'd give her a hand with the fires and stuff first.'

'Right. I'm going to see if Gran's got any cake we can take with us,' Billy said, as they slid down the enormous curved banister that connected their tiny attic room with the large hallway downstairs. 'Or some of them chocolate biscuits.'

'Good thinking. Though I expect Meatball's mum will have a load to eat.'

'Any idea what he wants? Meatball, I mean?'

Spike laughed. 'Oh, you know Meatball, he'll eat anything.'

'*No*, not that, I mean why he's called the meeting.'

Spike shook his head. 'He didn't really say. Just said he'd got some news.'

A loud ring at the bell interrupted their conversation.

'Hello, who's that?'

Rushing into the sitting-room, they peered around the curtain. Gran had opened the door and on the step stood a very large, square man, in a thick, fur-collared coat and broad hat.

'Who's he?'

'Don't know,' said Billy. 'I can't see his face. He looks familiar, though. Got a feeling I've seen him before.'

Spike squinted in the sunlight. 'Me, too.'

They stared long and hard at the man, who stepped slightly back to look at the window.

Quickly letting go of the curtain, they listened as Gran opened the door.

'It's that guy that was at Gullivan's place last year,' Spike said. 'When we were in there trying to find the crystal for Mr Price! He arrived with that woman!'

'That horrible woman with the big earrings? Yeah, I remember!'

They looked at one another. '*The gangsters!*' they said, together.

'Wonder what they want?'

Spike leaned a little closer to the window, but without moving the curtain it was difficult to see. They stood very still, listening to the mumble of words. The man's shape turned and walked back down the path.

Very carefully, Spike lifted the edge of the curtain. 'He's going back to the car.'

Billy squeezed in beside him to watch as the man wrenched on the car door. A slender woman stepped out, and pushed her way past him. She was wrapped in furs and wearing the most ridiculous boots. Her hair was longer now and swept up into a hat, but they knew her at once.

'It's her!' Billy hissed. 'It's the woman!'

'What does she want?'

The man moved to the back of the car and lifted an enormous hatch door. Out onto the snow jumped a big dog. It was the same dog they'd seen another man walking through the snow that day: the man who had burst into the waiting room on the hunt for Gullivan.

The square man in the coat and hat grabbed the dog's lead and, together with the woman, started to walk down the path towards their front door, the huge dog lumbering along beside them through the snow.

From behind the edge of the curtain, Spike saw another man get out of the car, walk round, and shut the hatch.

He grabbed Billy's arm. 'Quick, Bill,' he said. 'Gran might need our help.'

They darted out into the hallway.

'Yeah, that's fine,' the woman was saying. 'I'm just glad to get rid of it.'

Thrusting the lead into Gran's hand, she turned and stomped back up the path, slipping and sliding in her heels.

The man gave a last glance back at Gran. 'Thank you, Mrs Makepeace,' he said. He bent down to pat the dog. 'You'll be better off here, boy,' he murmured. 'Have a nice life.'

Then he followed the woman down the path.

Back at the car, the woman settled herself in the back. 'Well, shut the door then, you useless article!' she shrieked. Without replying, the square man shut the door behind her.

Gran watched for a moment and then closed their own front door very firmly.

'You all right, Gran?'

She swung around, smiling. 'Yes, dear, everything's fine.' She looked down at the dog. 'Poor mite. He's right, you'll be better off here with us.'

Spike's heart leaped. 'Is he ours, Gran?'

Smiling, Gran held out the lead. 'He is now,' she said.

Bursting with joy, they rushed toward the dog and threw their arms around its neck.

'Oh,' said Gran, suddenly, 'how silly of me. I forgot to ask what his name was.'

'It's Mason!' yelled Billy.

'We know him,' said Spike, ruffling the dog's ears.

'So, you know him already?' Gran called from the kitchen. 'Well now, there's a coincidence.'

'That's not the only coincidence.'

Billy looked up at Spike. 'What is it?'

With a glance at the kitchen door, Spike bent down to whisper.

'Did you see who the other guy was? The one in the car? It was the guy back there at the old station. The one with the *gun*.'

Half an hour later, Terri, Spike and Billy walked through the slush of a thawing village square on their way to Meatball's house.

'And you're sure it was him?' Terri asked.

Spike nodded. 'I'd know him anywhere.'

'She must be his wife then.'

'Rather him than me.'

'He's horrible 'n' all,' Billy said.

'Wonder why he tried to shoot Gullivan?' Terri asked.

'Don't know. Don't care much, either.'

No one spoke of the train. Of all that had happened, Cornelius Gullivan in that train was the one thing none of them had mentioned, not to Gran or Mr Price.

Spike wasn't sure why, but he suspected that with the others, too, it was something to do with the uneasy feeling that engulfed them whenever they thought of it.

'Spike!'

He looked up. Duke and Doc were hurrying across the road to meet them.

'Come and look!' Duke cried. 'You've got to come and look at what we've found round here!'

They set off around the corner and into the High Street. Now the thaw had set in, people were venturing out and into the shops and the High Street was a brightly lit bustle of noise and colour.

'What is it?'

'Down here, look, at the end of the road. Last shop on the corner.'

Slipping and sliding along the pavement, they paused before a small shop at the end, closed temporarily for renovation. Scaffolding almost obscured the front and the pavement was partly blocked by a large skip and bits and pieces of rubble and building equipment.

Terri gazed at it. 'This one?'

Duke looked at them expectantly. 'Recognise it?'

'I do,' said Billy, at once. 'It's the shop where we rescued that couple.'

'Exactly!' said Doc. 'And amongst everything else, they're taking all the old signs down. Look.'

There were several signs dumped in the skip, and it was clear that at one time or another, the shop had been through a variety of uses.

With a quick glance behind, Duke stepped back off the kerb and into the road. 'Now look,' he said. 'Up there above the door. The old original wartime sign. It's got wartime adverts at either end.'

Spike looked up. And there it was, in somewhat faded lettering. "TYLERS HARDWARE."

'Tylers Hardware,' he read. '*Tyler*?'

He stared at Duke. 'You're kidding me! Not ... not the same Tyler. It can't be.'

'It probably isn't,' said Terri. 'Tyler's a common surname. Could be anyone.'

'No, it isn't,' Doc said, quietly. 'I've checked with the owners. They own the one next door as well. That's what they're doing, joining the two together. And I asked them did they know anything about the previous owners. They told me that during the war, it was owned by a Mr and Mrs Tyler and their granddaughter still lives in the village, and I might know the great-grandson. His name's Brett.'

Terri's mouth gaped. 'So ... so the couple we rescued ...'

'Were Brett's great-grandparents,' said Billy.

'I don't be*lieve* it,' Spike moaned.

'Neither could we,' Duke muttered. 'But it's them, all right. Apparently, the tale about the plane hitting the roof during the war is now something of a legend round here. The story goes that they were helped by a group of children and two lizards.'

'Oh, dear,' said Terri, bluntly.

Duke shrugged. 'Not much we can do,' he said. 'There's no way we wouldn't have helped them, is there?'

'No,' said Spike, bitterly. 'No, course not. They were nice people. It's not their fault their great-grandson's a scumbag.'

'Wait till we tell Meatball!' Billy cried. 'And about Mason!'

'Mason?' Who's Mason?'

CHAPTER THIRTY-FOUR

'So you've got a new dog now? Mason?'

Spike grinned. 'Yup.'

They were sitting in the warmth of Meatball's basement, eating their way through a loaf of bread.

Meatball cheered. 'Yes!'

'Be much better off with you lot,' said Doc, thinking about the woman they'd seen the previous year. 'She was a nasty bit of goods.'

'So's he,' Terri remarked. 'They're horrible, both of them.'

'That's brilliant news,' said Duke. 'You still going to keep his name then?'

Billy nodded. 'Yeah,' he said, 'he's used to it.'

'Soon as he's settled in a bit, we can bring him over to meet Gus,' said Spike. 'Right, I'll do some more toast, while you tell Meatball about the shop. You got to hear this, Meatball, you haven't heard anything yet.'

He slid two slices of toast onto forks and held them over the fire.

'What shop?'

'We found it,' said Duke. 'We found the shop that got hit by the plane.'

'You mean the one where we rescued those two people?'

'Yep.'

'It's still there, then?'

'Yep,' said Duke, again. '*And...*'

He accepted a slice of toast from Doc, who was buttering slices as fast as Spike could toast them. 'And,' he said, biting his toast with a crunch, 'you'll never guess who those people were.' A dribble of butter ran down his chin. 'That couple we rescued were only Brett Tyler's great-grandparents, weren't they?'

'You're having a laugh.'

'No,' said Doc. 'They really were. And *we* are now a legend.'

'A *living* legend,' said Billy. 'Though no one else knows that. Except for Mr Judd, of course.'

'On the downside, they thought Jo and Neez were lizard-people,' said Terri.

Meatball pulled a face. 'Well, I s'pose that's understandable,' he said. 'But we won't tell them. So ... Brett Tyler ...'

He huffed. 'Typical, that is. Still, they were all right, it's just him that's a creep.'

Doc passed him some toast. 'That's what we said. You can't blame them for having such a revolting great-grandson.'

'So,' said Spike, 'what is it you've got to tell us then, Meatball? You said you had some news.'

'Oh!' Meatball licked butter from his fingers. 'Yes. Well, first of all, there's this. Mum was up in the loft yesterday sorting through some stuff and she came across it.'

Wiping his hands on his jeans, he stretched a long arm across to the desk opposite and picked up a book. A coloured sticky note protruded from the pages.

Laying the book down in front of them, he slipped his fingers under the page and opened it. 'Have a look there,' he said, mysteriously. 'See anyone you know?'

They scrutinised the old photographs on the page.

'It's her!' Billy suddenly cried, pointing towards a small photo in the corner. 'It's the woman who helped us! In the war!'

'Oh, wow! So it is!'

'It *is* her!' Duke looked up at Meatball, whose face was shining with pleasure. 'Who is she then, Meatball?'

'You'll never believe it,' he said, smiling fit to burst, 'I asked Mum. That's her nan. *My* great-grandmother.'

'So that's why you felt you knew her.' Terri gazed at the photo, wonderingly. 'There's a definite resemblance ... around the eyes.'

Meatball nodded furiously. 'I know. I suppose I must've seen a bit of Nan and Mum in her face – and the way she walked - but course, I never actually met her. And Mum said she was in the forces during the war *and*, you remember I said about her legs?

'You said there was something odd about them?'

'Yes. Well, it was lines, wasn't it? I even remembered myself after. They used to draw lines ...'

'Down their legs,' Doc interrupted. 'They used to draw lines down their legs when they didn't have any stockings.'

'That's right!' said Terri. 'I remember my Nan saying about that. Stockings were in short supply during the war so they used to dye their legs when they went out and draw a line down them with eyebrow pencil, because in those days stockings had seams down the back.'

'It explains the uniform, as well,' said Doc. 'You said the woman was wearing a uniform, didn't you? So, it was your great-nan all the time. Mystery solved. I'm so glad, Meatball. Sounds silly, but I'm kind of glad she was there.'

Meatball smiled. 'Yes,' he said. 'And me. Wish I could've ... well, you know ... said thank you.'

'And us,' said Duke. 'Maybe she knows, eh?'

With a wistful look, Meatball put the book away. 'Yeah,' he said. 'Maybe she does.'

They munched quietly on through slices of toast for several minutes, before anyone said more.

'So, what else is it, Meatball?'

Just about to take another bite, Meatball paused and glanced across at Spike. 'What?'

'Well, just now, you said, 'First of all.'

'Did I?'

'Uh-huh.'

A strange look crept across Meatball's face. A troubled look that said he was worried about something, and wanted to share it, but didn't know whether to.

'What's up, Meatball? Come on, you can tell us.'

Meatball shuffled about in his seat. 'I didn't say anything before,' he said, 'because it was only once and I thought … but I've had it again, now. The same dream. Twice. And it's really vivid and I can't shake it off.'

'Oh, hell,' said Spike.

To anyone else it would mean nothing, but to Meatball's friends, the fact that he was having vivid dreams again was not good news. Meatball had had the same nightmare for months before their first adventure the previous year, Spike remembered, and things happened just as he'd predicted.

'Maybe it's just a dream,' said Terri, reassuringly. 'Maybe it's just coincidence.'

'We seem to have a lot of coincidences,' Doc said quietly.

'Oh, hell,' said Spike, again.

'You'd better tell us about it,' said Billy.

'Don't know if that's a good idea.'

'That bad?'

'Tell us, Meatball,' said Duke. 'We've got to know anyway.'

'*Tell* us,' Spike said.

Meatball closed his eyes and tried to think. 'It's still a mess at the moment, you know, like they start off, all bits and pieces that don't make any sense …'

He opened his eyes. 'But the bit that's worrying me is *him.*'

'Who?'

Meatball took a breath. '*Gullivan*,' he said.

**Don't Miss the first exciting instalment of
The Yew Tree Chronicles**

What would you do if you suspected a family
friend was missing?
Spike is worried about Joseph Price. He hasn't
been seen for several days and Spike is sure his
evil neighbour, Cornelius Gullivan has something
to do with it. Spike's friends are not convinced.
Until his dog digs up a bone on Gullivan's land.
The discovery plunges Spike and his friends into
the adventure of a lifetime in a prehistoric world,
where they have a fantastic enounter with an
ancient race. An ancient race that need their help.
Can they save their new friends in time?

Printed in Great Britain
by Amazon

18492266R00123